D1258415

The Super Adventures of
OLLIE
AND
BEA

SQUEALS ON WHEELS

Here's Bea and her best friend, Oll—

HEY! WAIT A MINUTE!
WHERE'S OLLIE?

RENÉE TREML

PICTURE WINDOW BOOKS
a capstone imprint

Published by Picture Window Books, an imprint of Capstone.
1710 Roe Crest Drive, North Mankato, Minnesota 56003
capstonepub.com

Library of Congress Cataloging-in-Publication Data
Names: Treml, Renée, author. | Treml, Renée, author.
Title: Squeals on wheels / Renée Treml.
Description: North Mankato, Minnesota : Picture Window Books, [2022] |
   Series: The super adventures of Ollie and Bea | Audience: Ages 5-7 | Audience:
   Grades K-1 |
Summary: "Ollie is having a hoot on his roller skates-but Bea is full of excuses
   for why she can not join in. Will Bea realize that real friends do not mind if you
   sometimes look silly?"-- Provided by publisher.
Identifiers: LCCN 2021043789 (print) | LCCN 2021043790 (ebook) |
   ISBN 9781666314892 (hardcover) | ISBN 9781666330915 (paperback) |
   ISBN 9781666330922 (pdf) | ISBN 9781666330946 (kindle edition)
Subjects: CYAC: Graphic novels. | Humorous stories. | Owls--Fiction. | Rabbits--
   Fiction. | Friendship--Fiction. | LCGFT: Funny animal comics. | Graphic novels.
Classification: LCC PZ7.7.T73 Sq 2022 (print) | LCC PZ7.7.T73 (ebook) | DDC
   741.5/994--dc23
LC record available at https://lccn.loc.gov/2021043789
LC ebook record available at https://lccn.loc.gov/2021043790

Designed by Kay Fraser

Printed and bound in the USA. 4608

TABLE OF CONTENTS

CHAPTER 1

OWL BE BACK

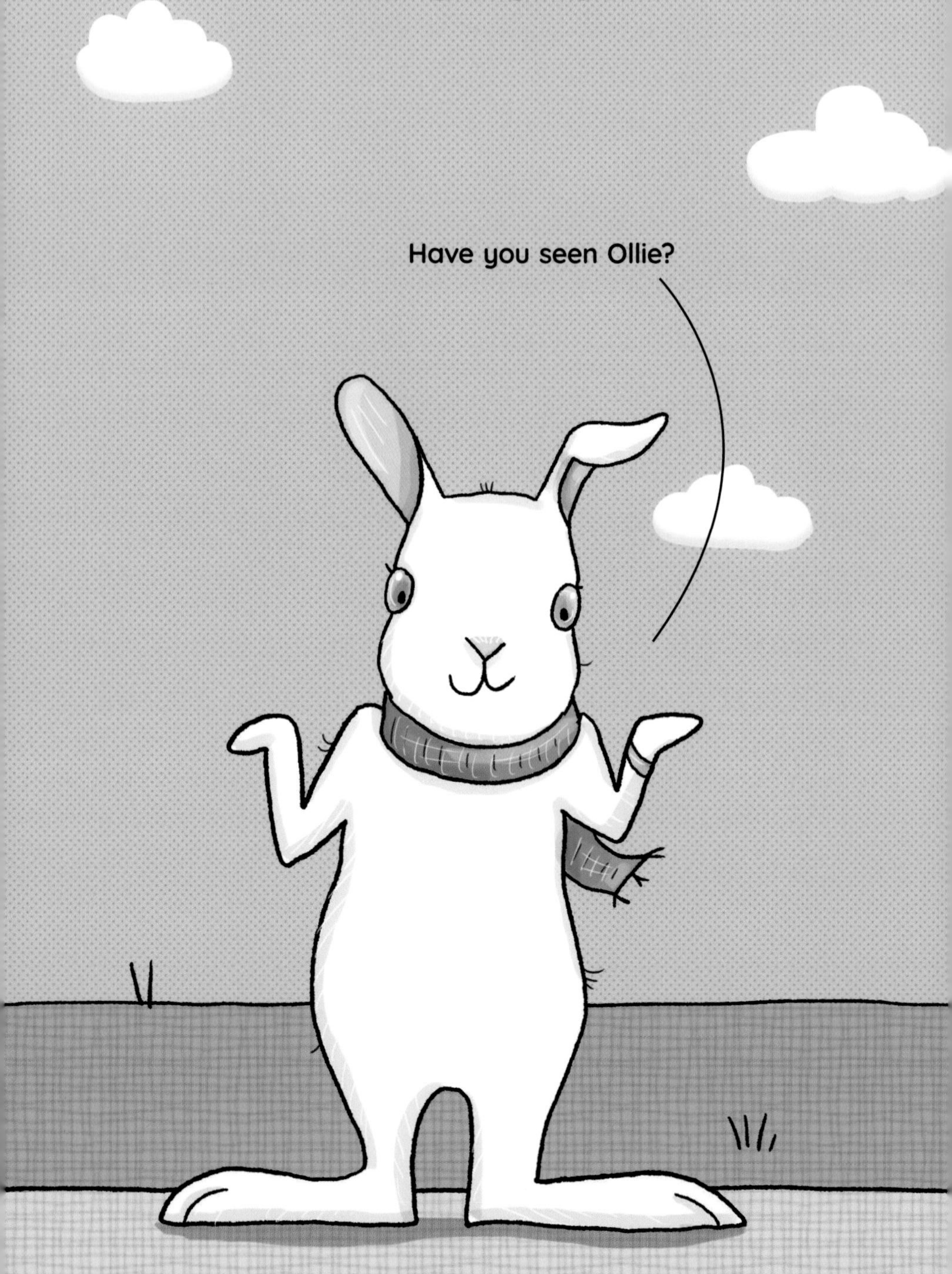
Have you seen Ollie?

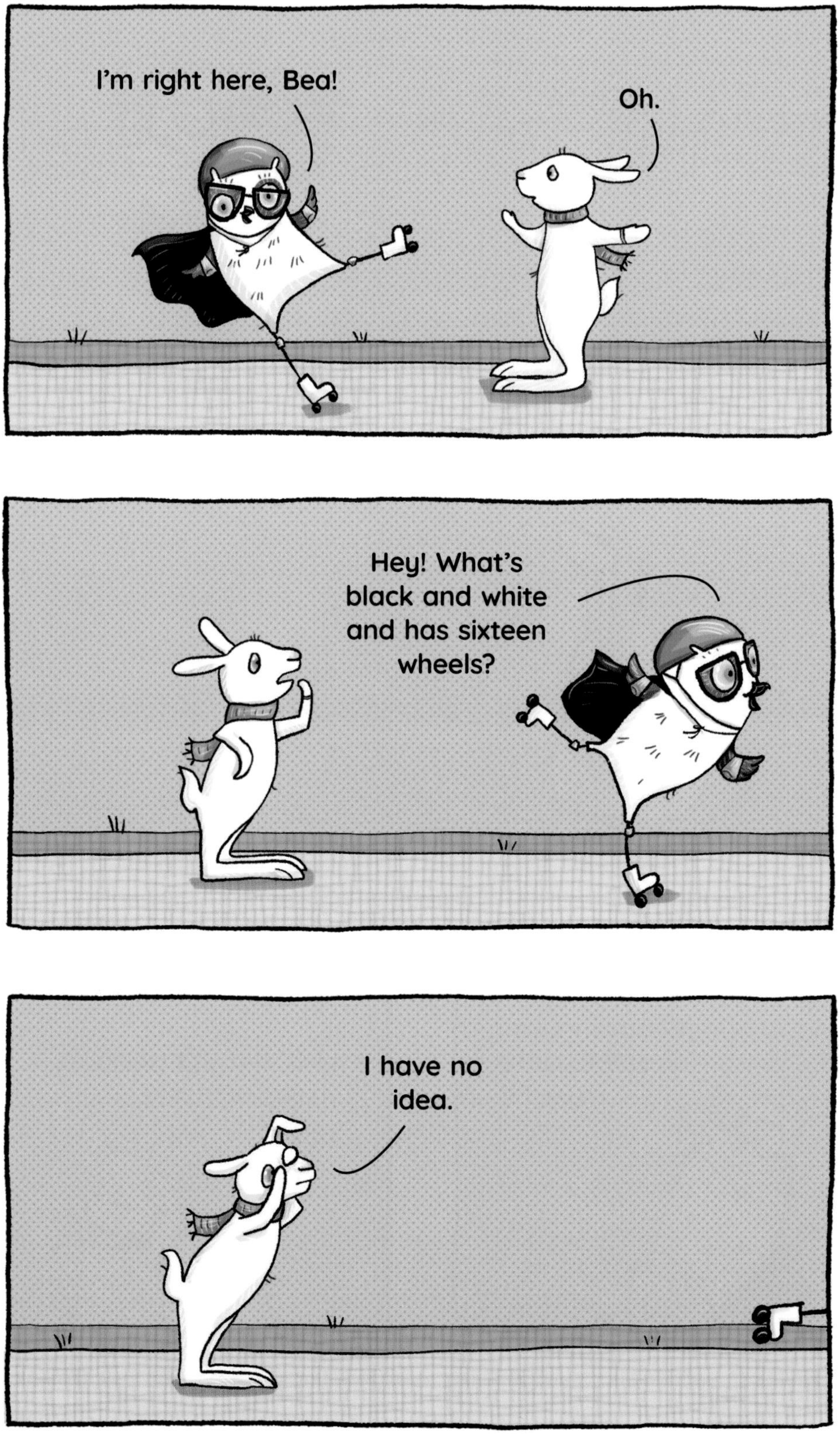
I'm right here, Bea!
Oh.
Hey! What's black and white and has sixteen wheels?
I have no idea.

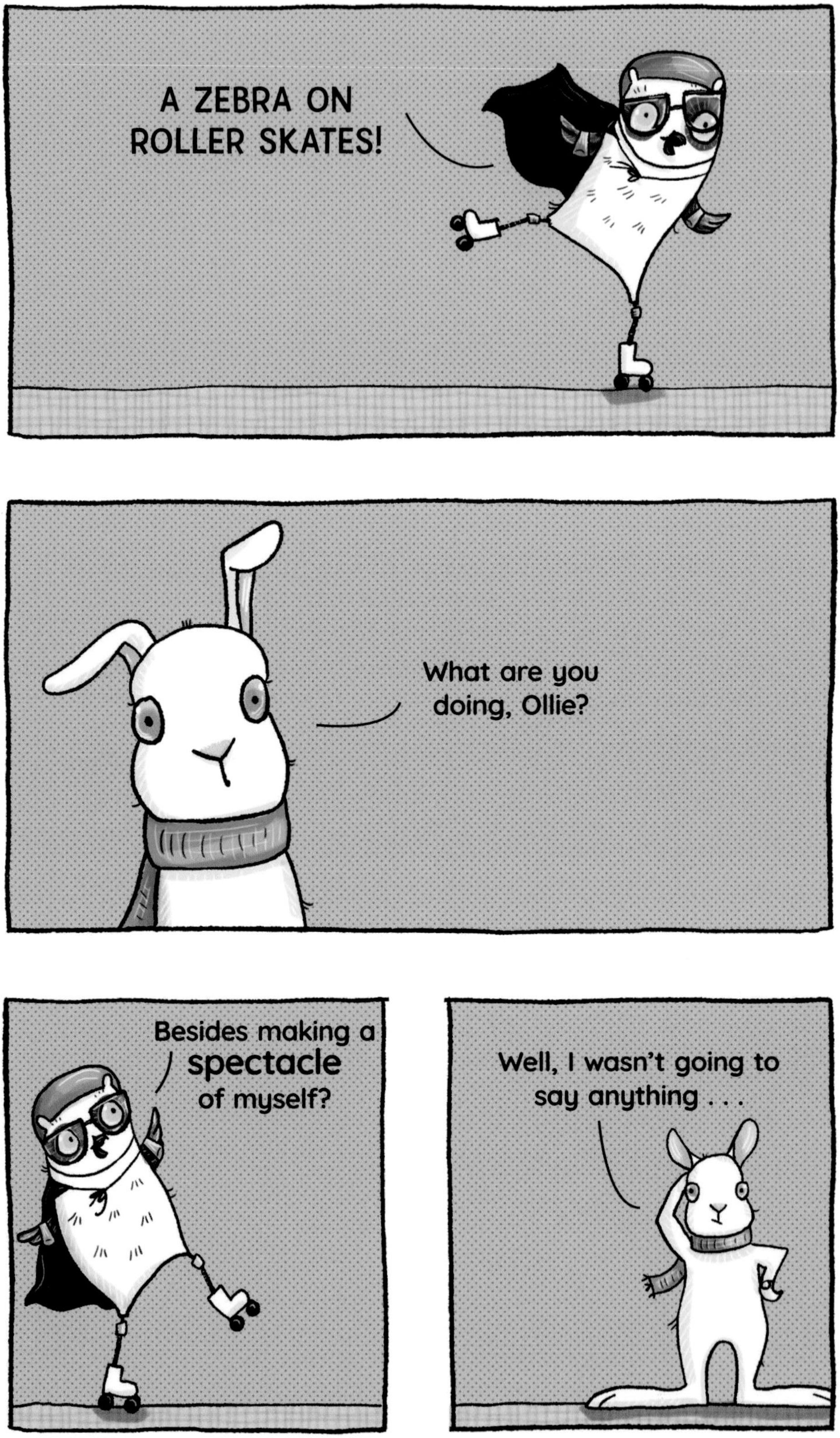
A ZEBRA ON ROLLER SKATES!
What are you doing, Ollie?
Besides making a spectacle of myself?
Well, I wasn't going to say anything . . .

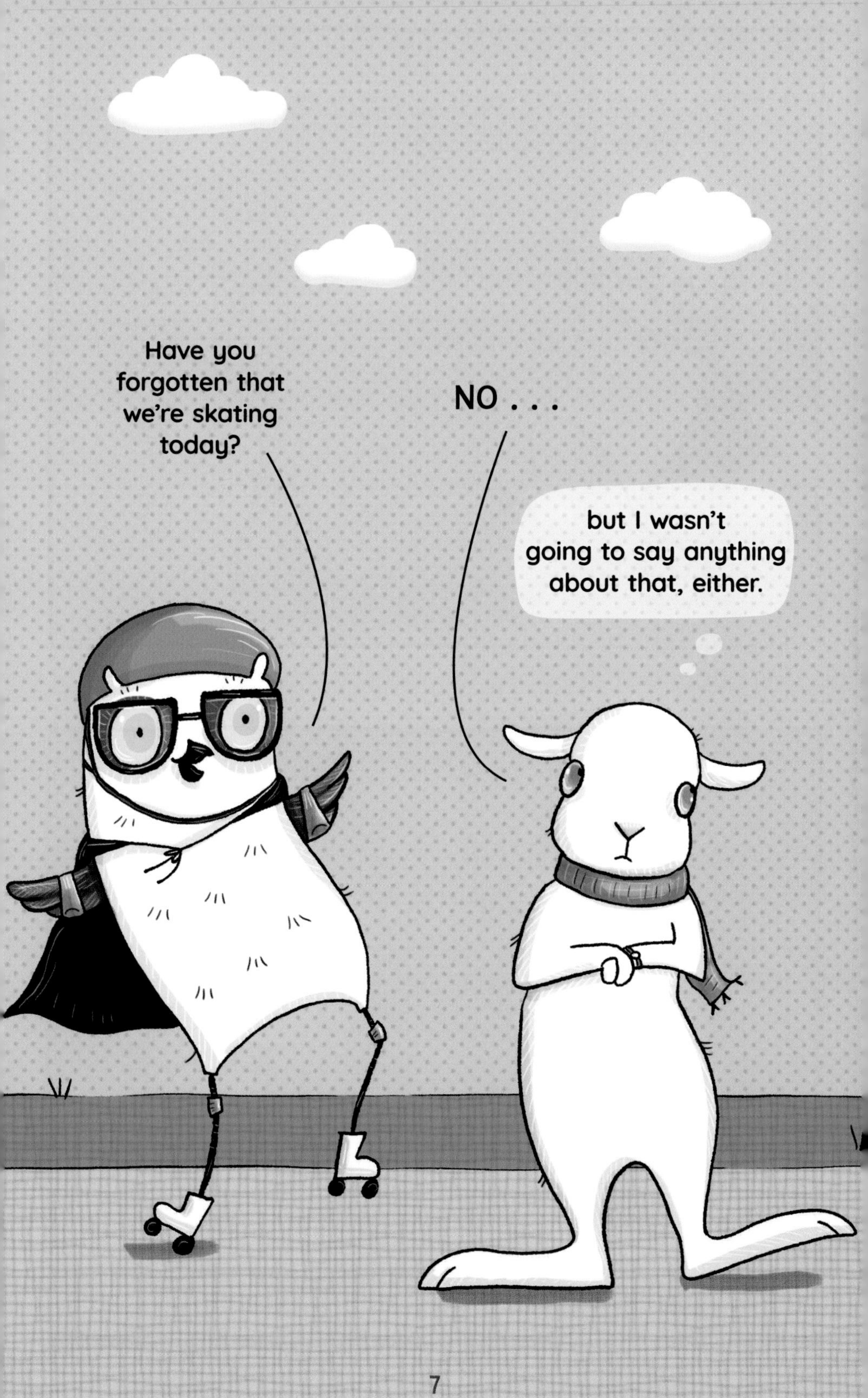
Have you forgotten that we're skating today?
NO . . .
but I wasn't going to say anything about that, either.

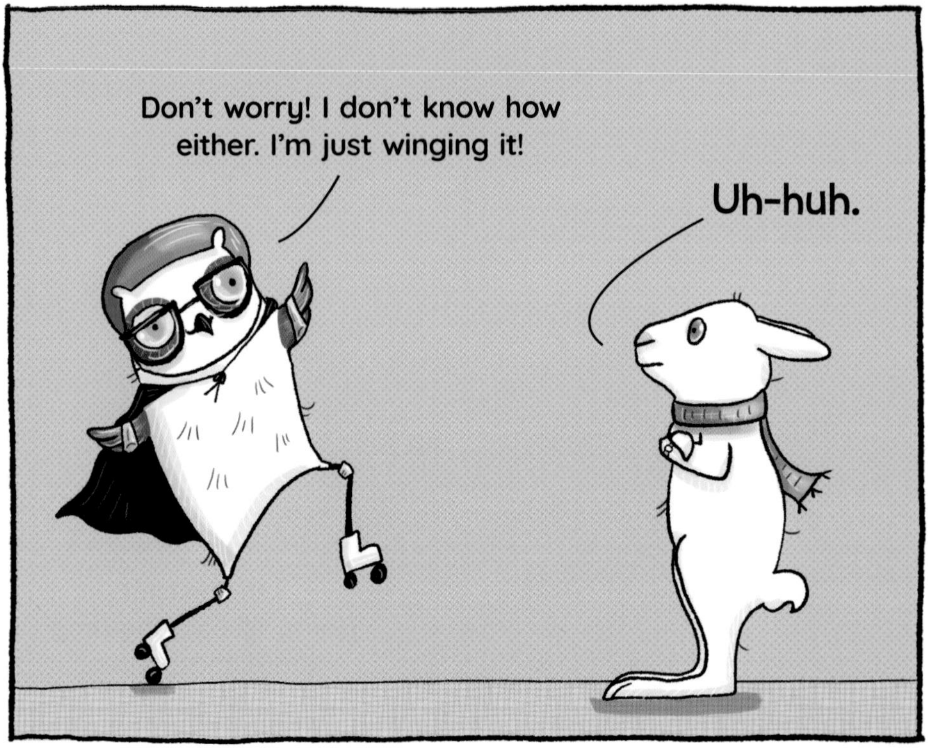
Don't worry! I don't know how either. I'm just winging it!
Uh-huh.

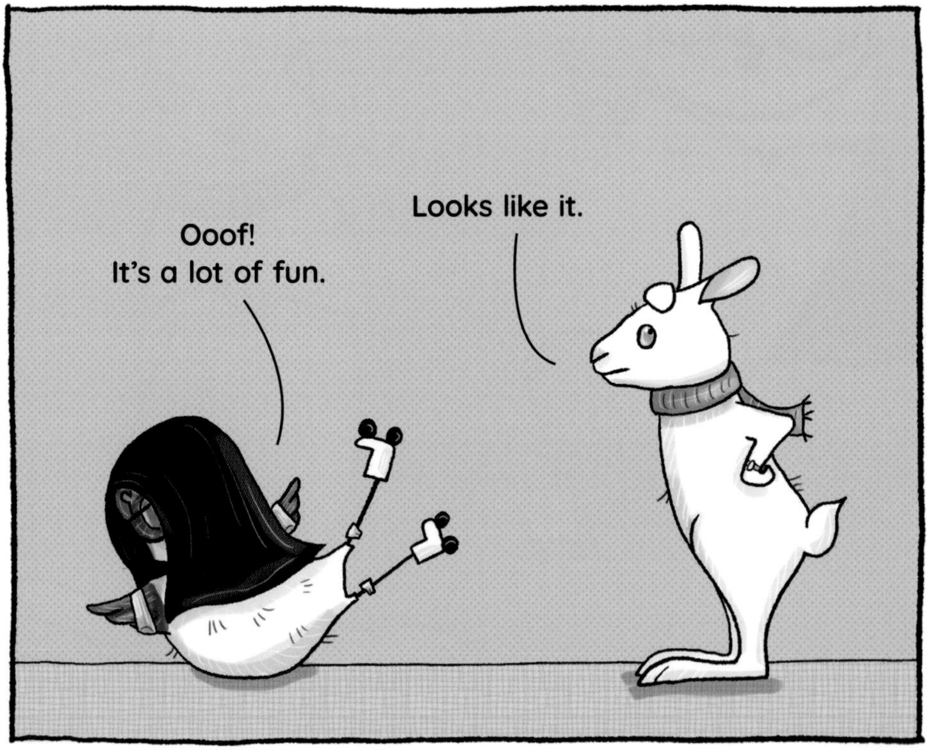
Ooof! It's a lot of fun.
Looks like it.

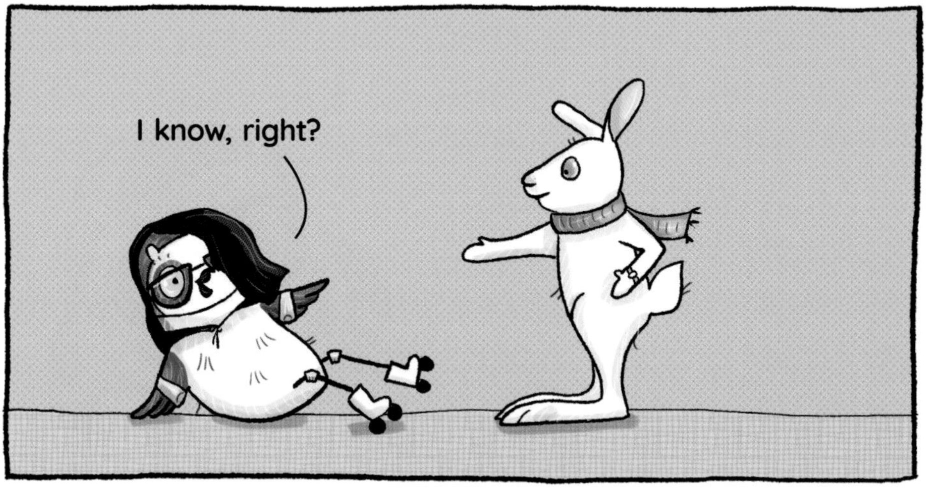
I know, right?

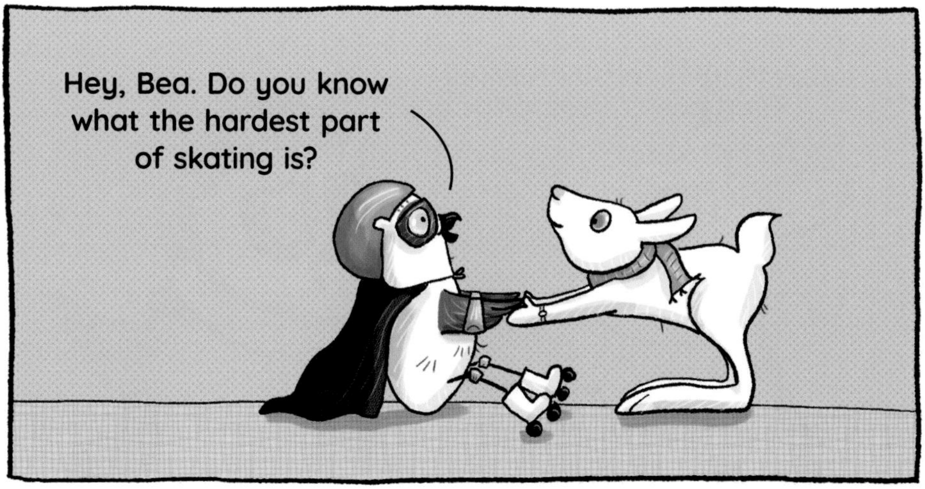
Hey, Bea. Do you know what the hardest part of skating is?

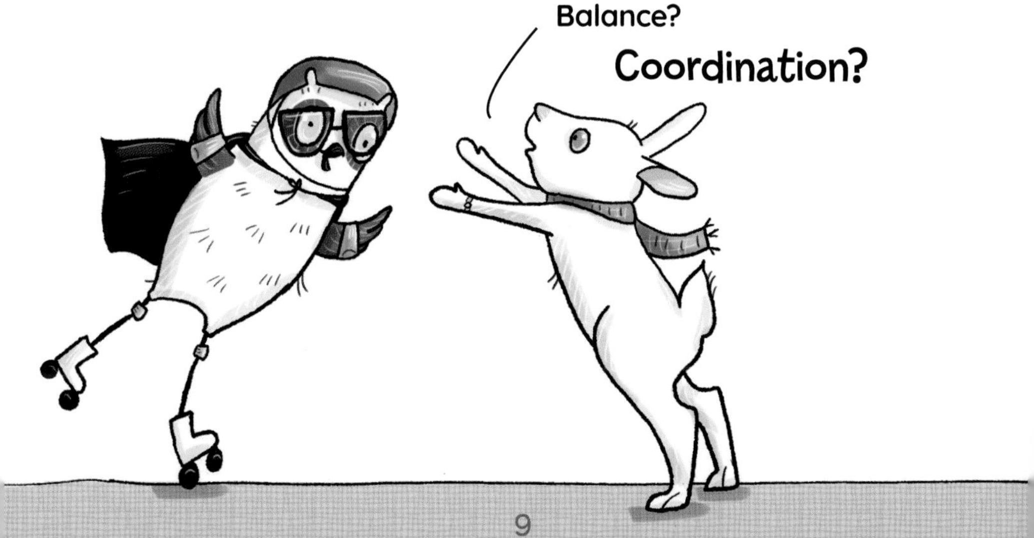
Balance?
Coordination?

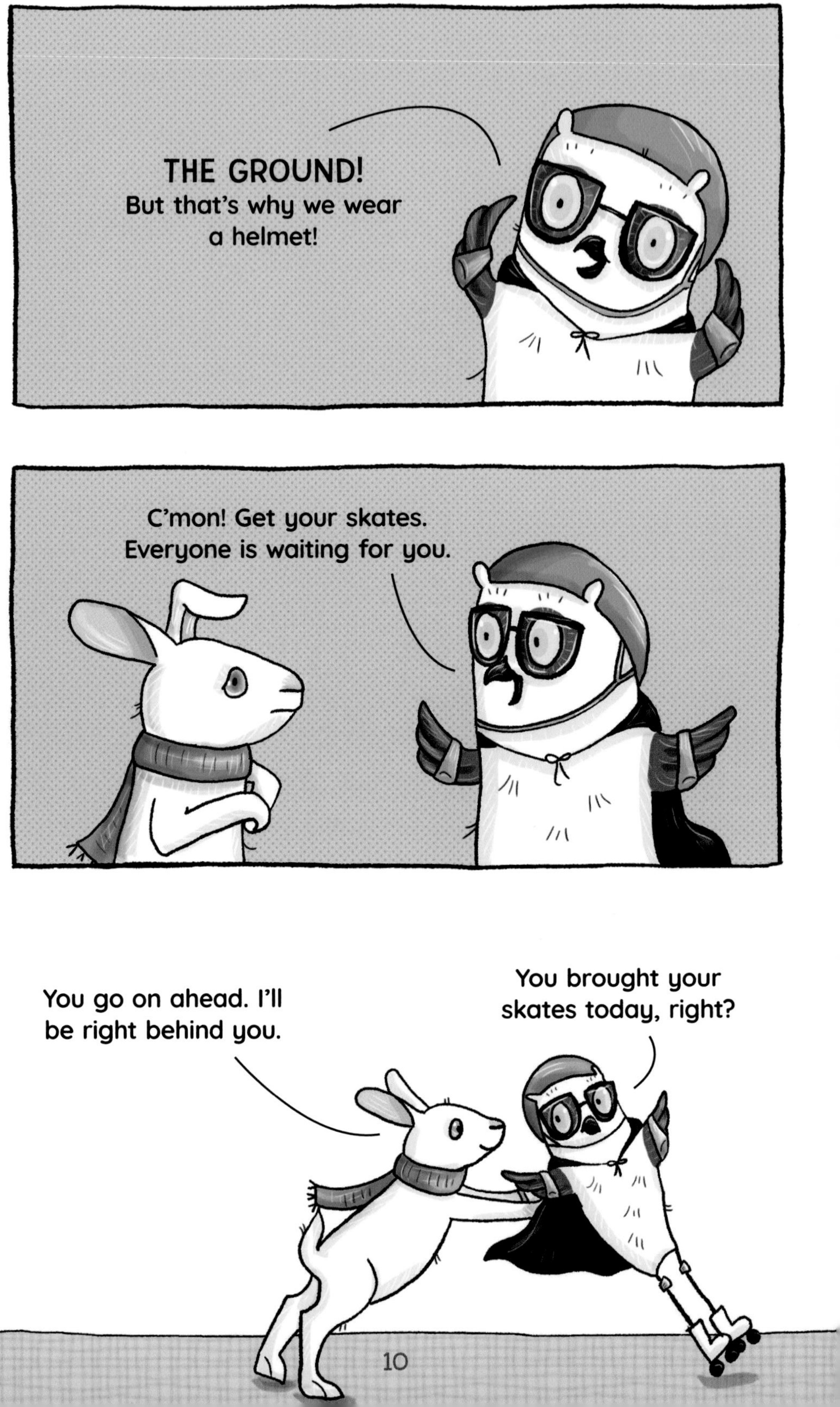
THE GROUND!
But that's why we wear a helmet!
C'mon! Get your skates. Everyone is waiting for you.
You brought your skates today, right?
You go on ahead. I'll be right behind you.

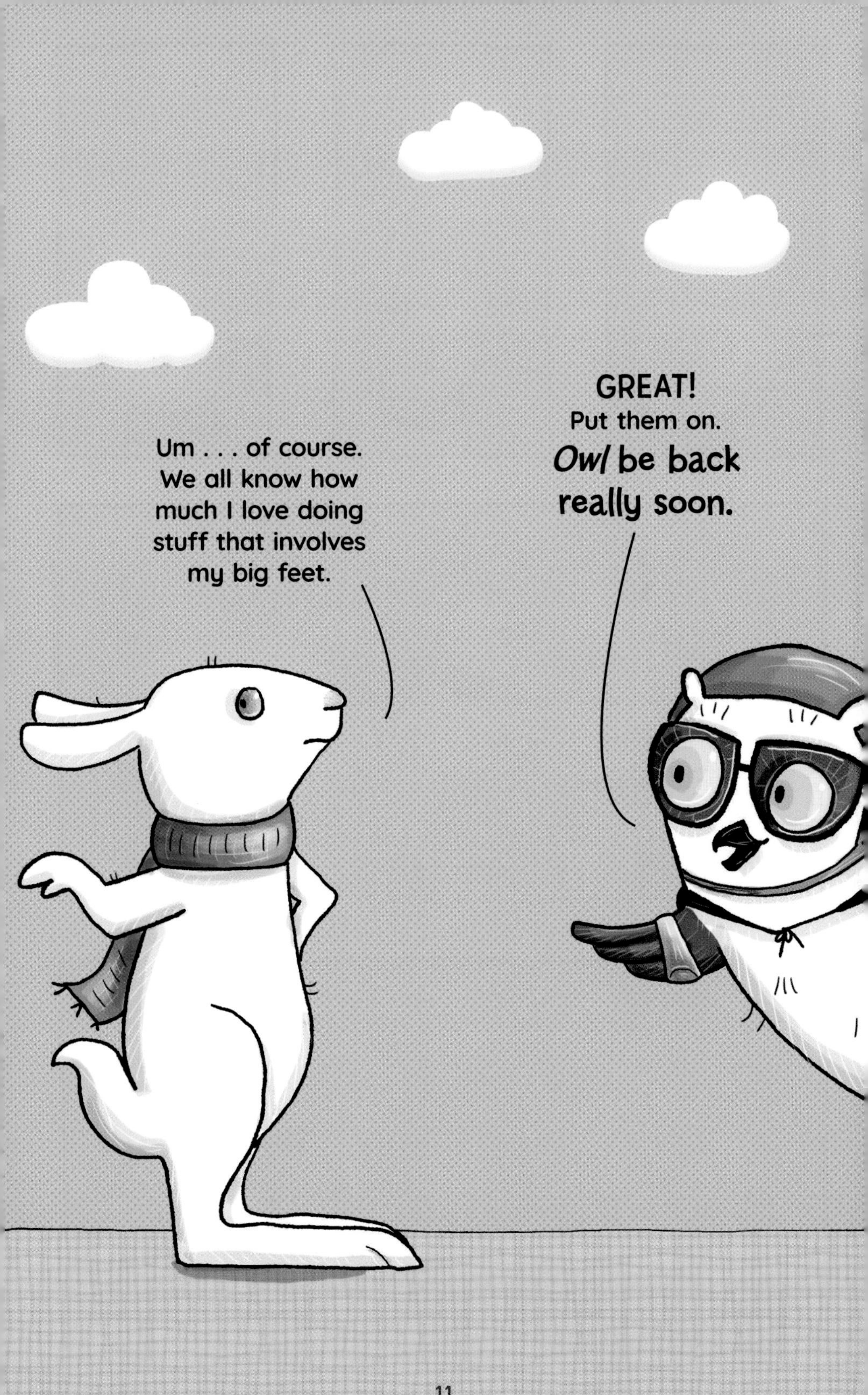
Um . . . of course. We all know how much I love doing stuff that involves my big feet.
GREAT! Put them on. *Owl* be back really soon.

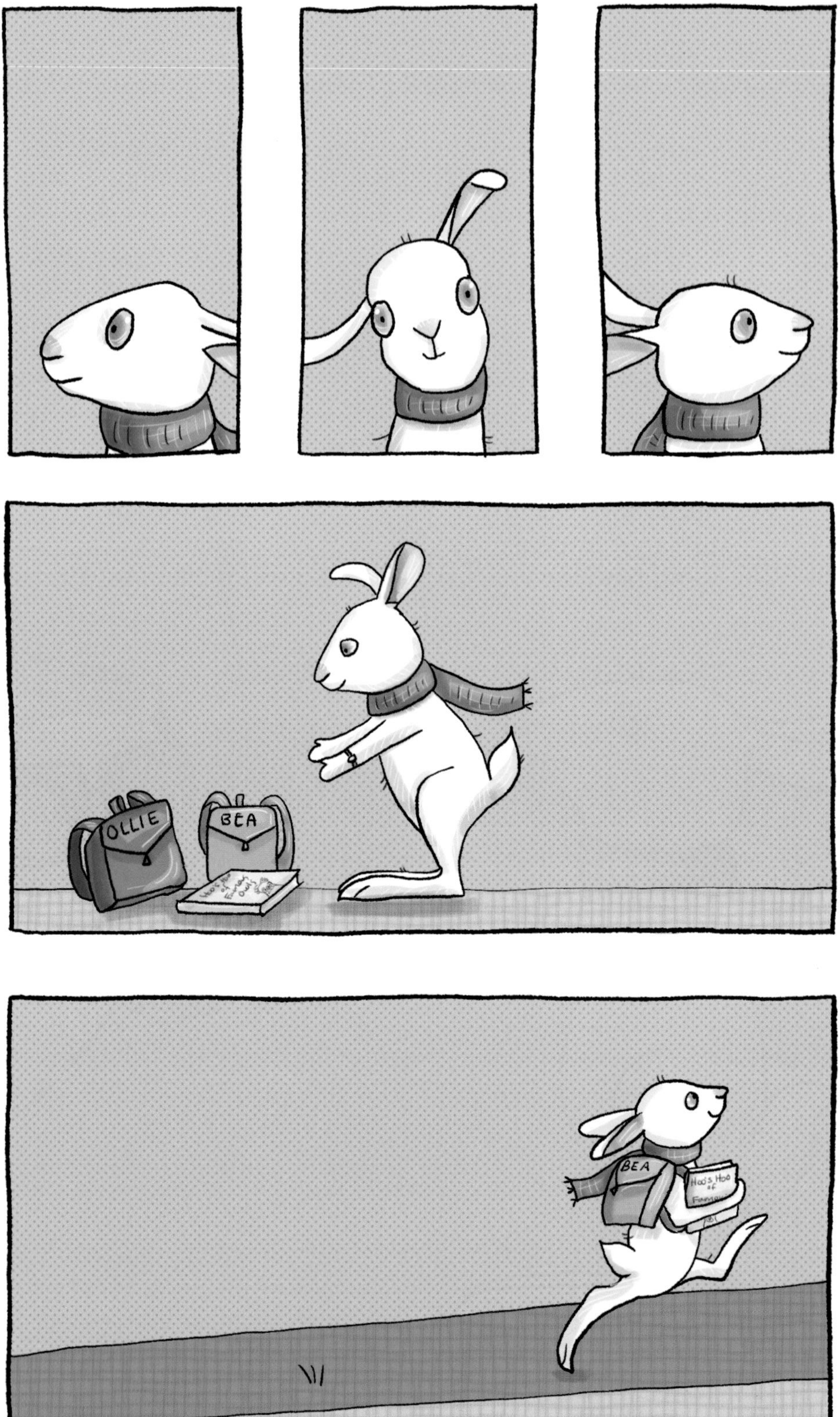
OLLIE
BEA
BEA

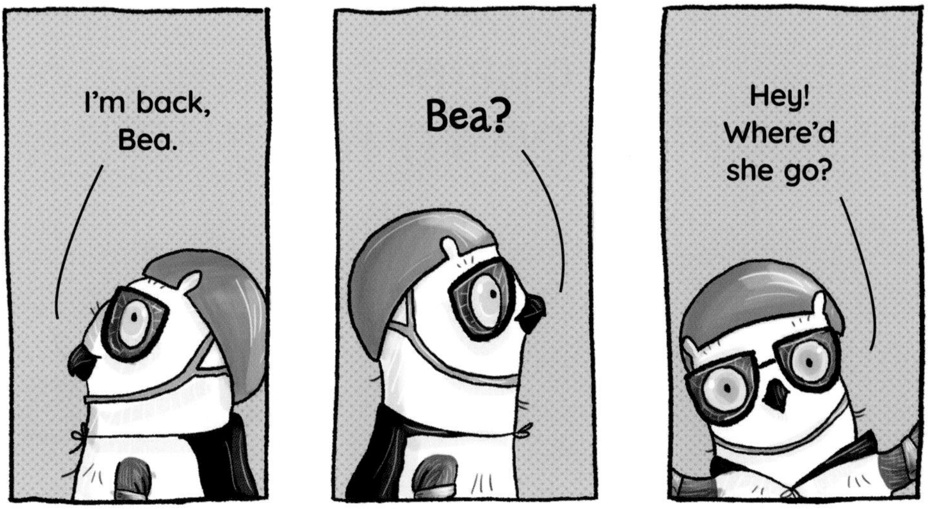
I'm back, Bea.
Bea?
Hey! Where'd she go?

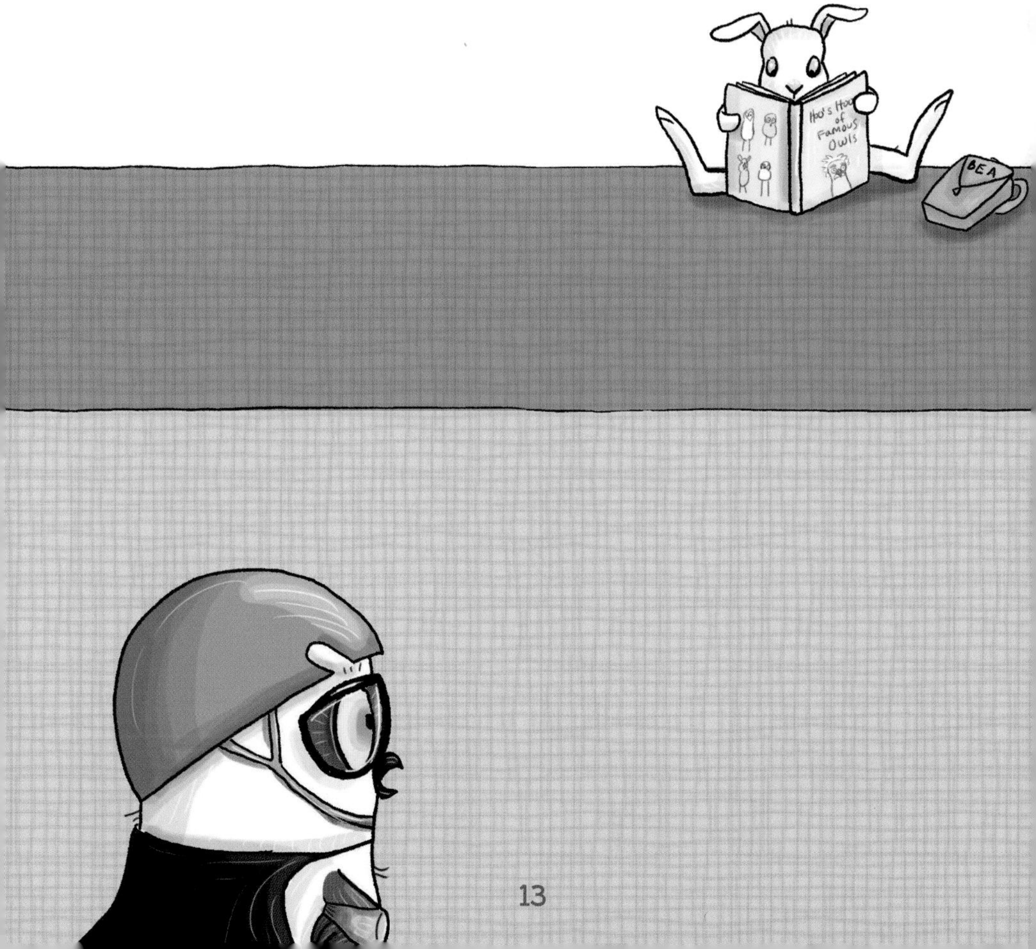
Hoo's Hoo of Famous Owls
BEA

CHAPTER 2

HOP TO IT

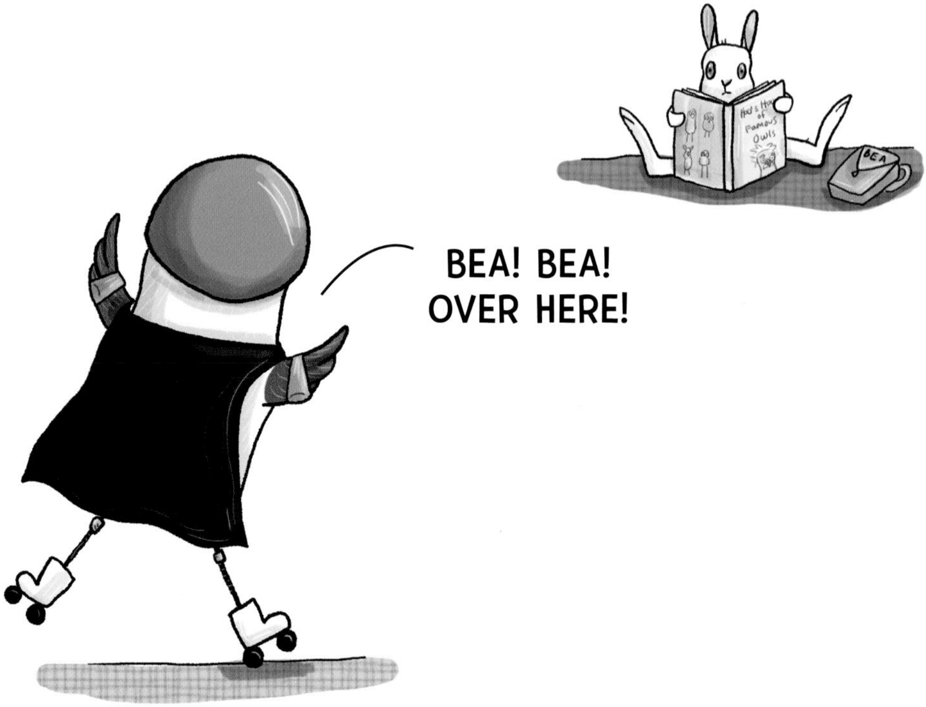

BEA! BEA! OVER HERE!

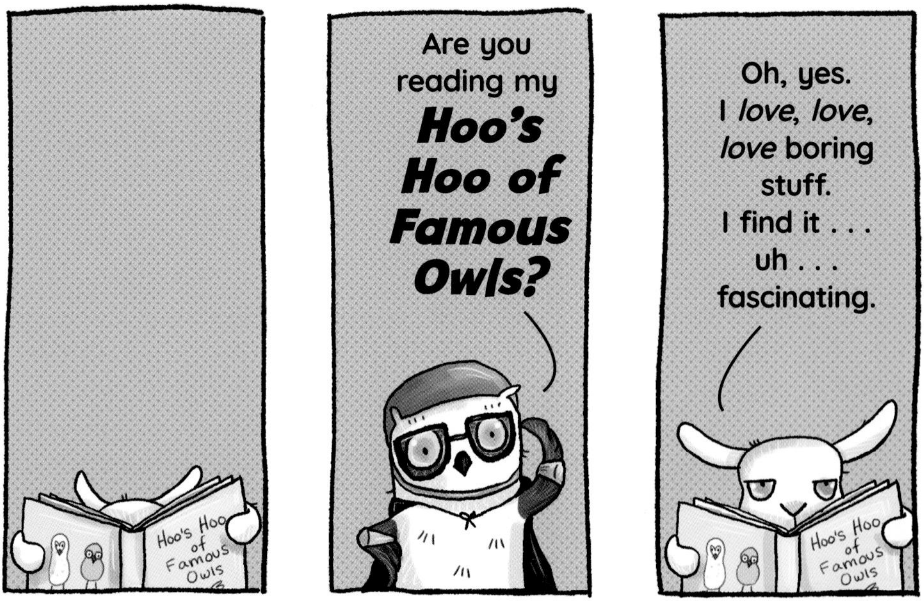

Are you reading my *Hoo's Hoo of Famous Owls?*
Oh, yes. I *love, love, love* boring stuff. I find it . . . uh . . . fascinating.

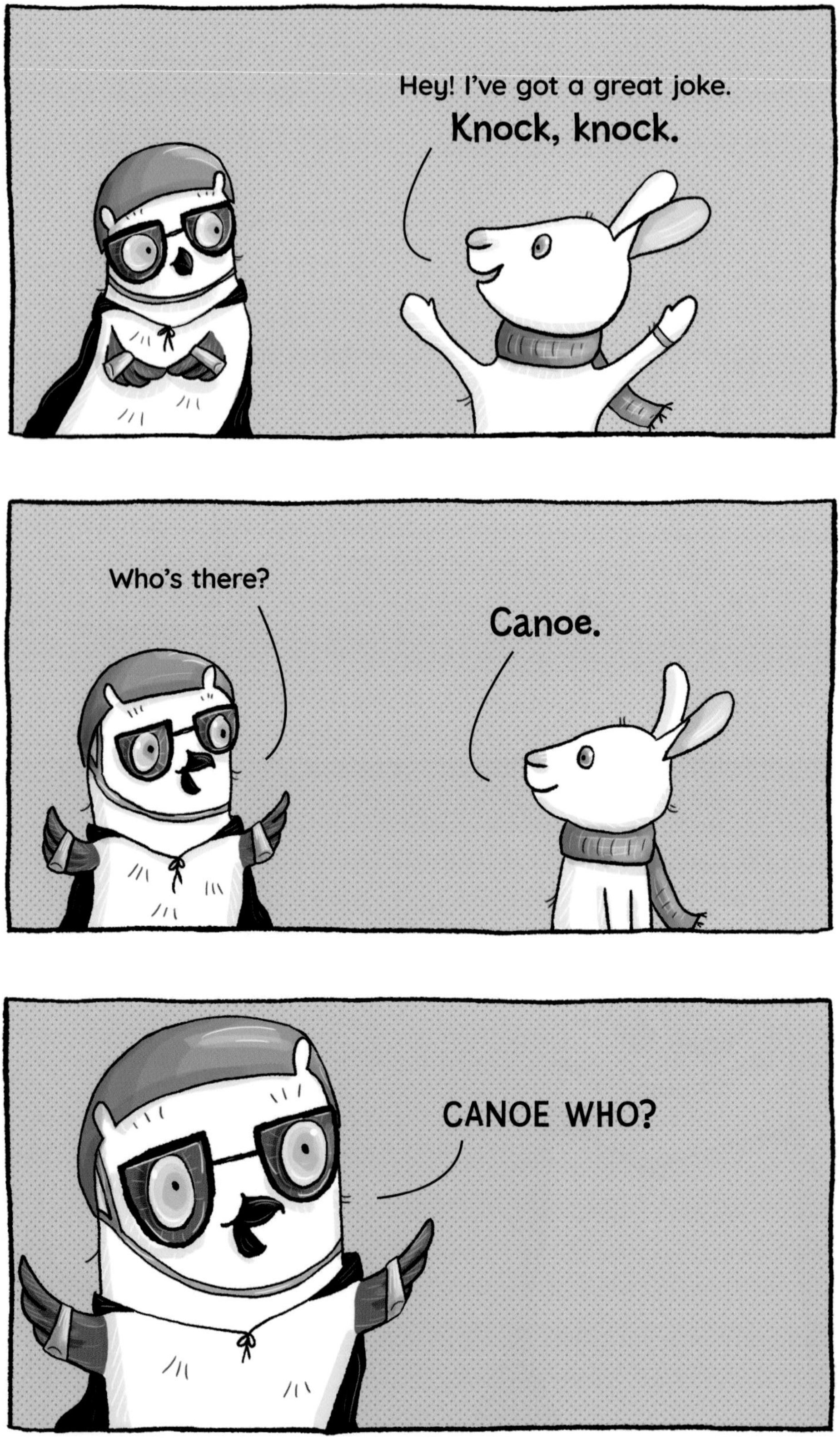

Hey! I've got a great joke.
Knock, knock.
Who's there?
Canoe.
CANOE WHO?

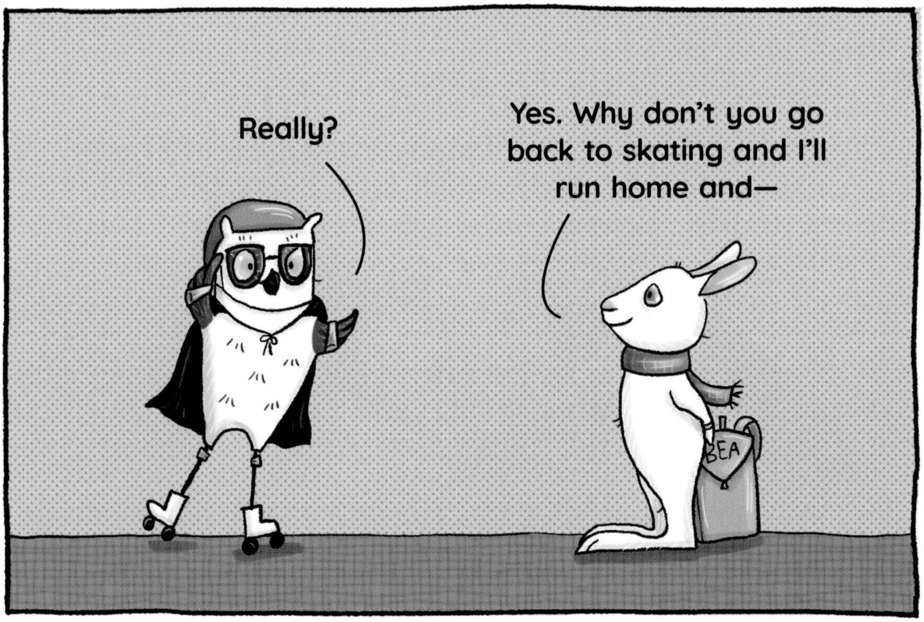
Really?
Yes. Why don't you go back to skating and I'll run home and—
BEA

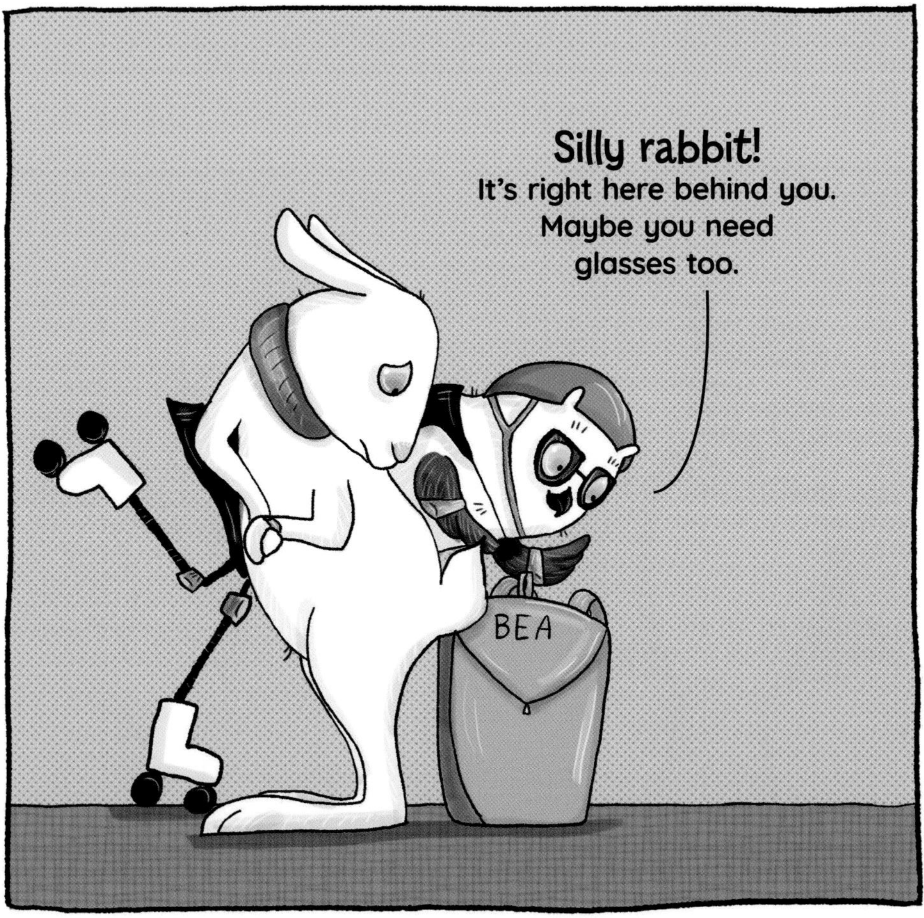
Silly rabbit!
It's right here behind you. Maybe you need glasses too.
BEA

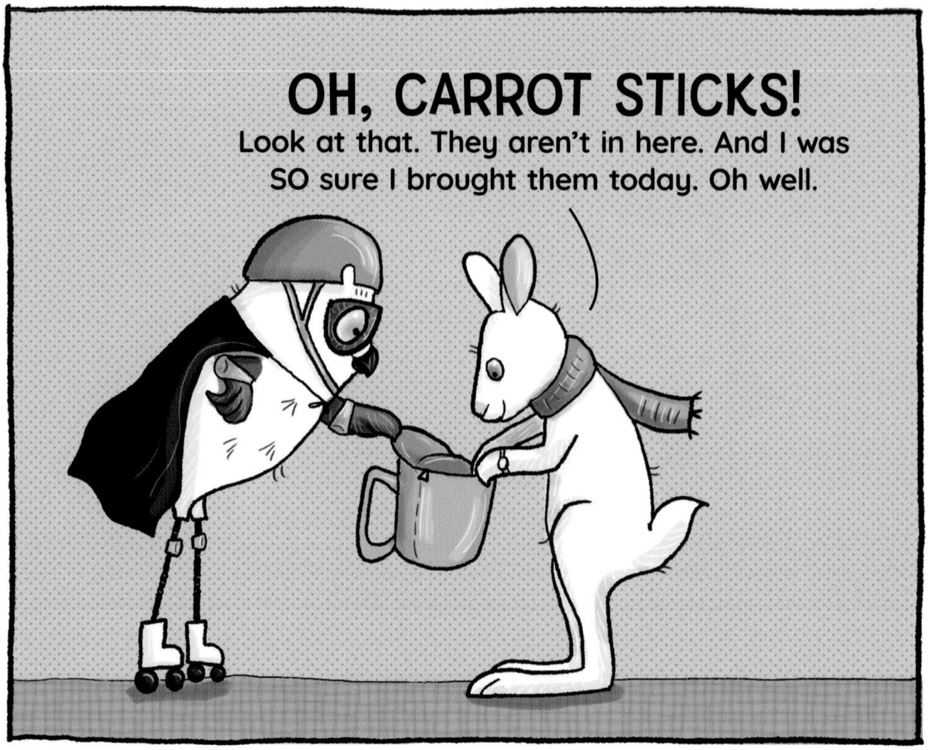
OH, CARROT STICKS!
Look at that. They aren't in here. And I was SO sure I brought them today. Oh well.

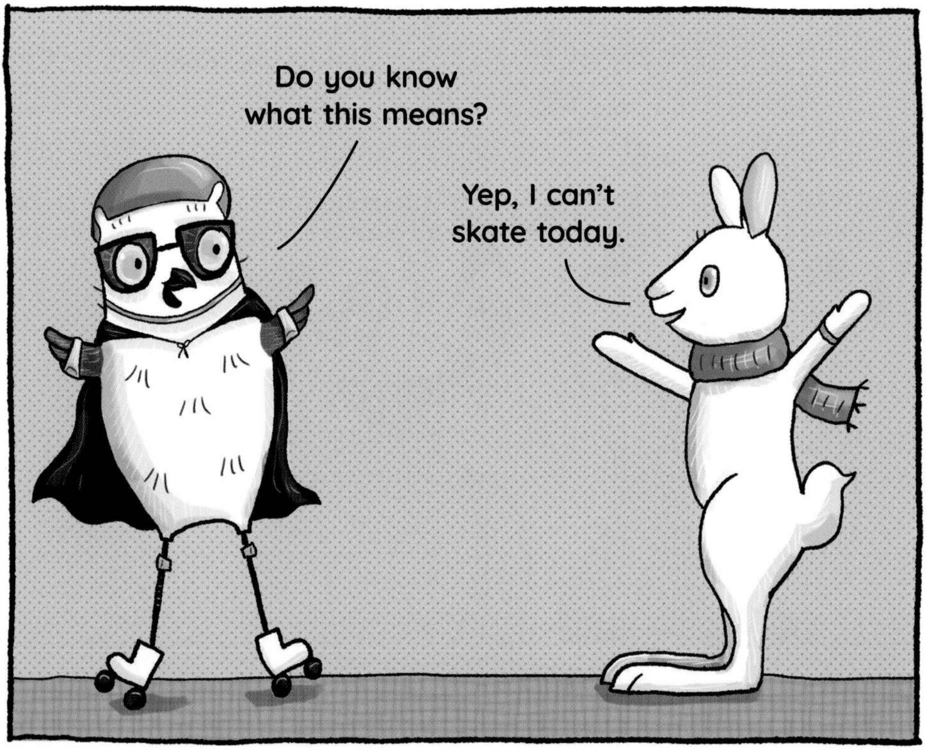
Do you know what this means?
Yep, I can't skate today.

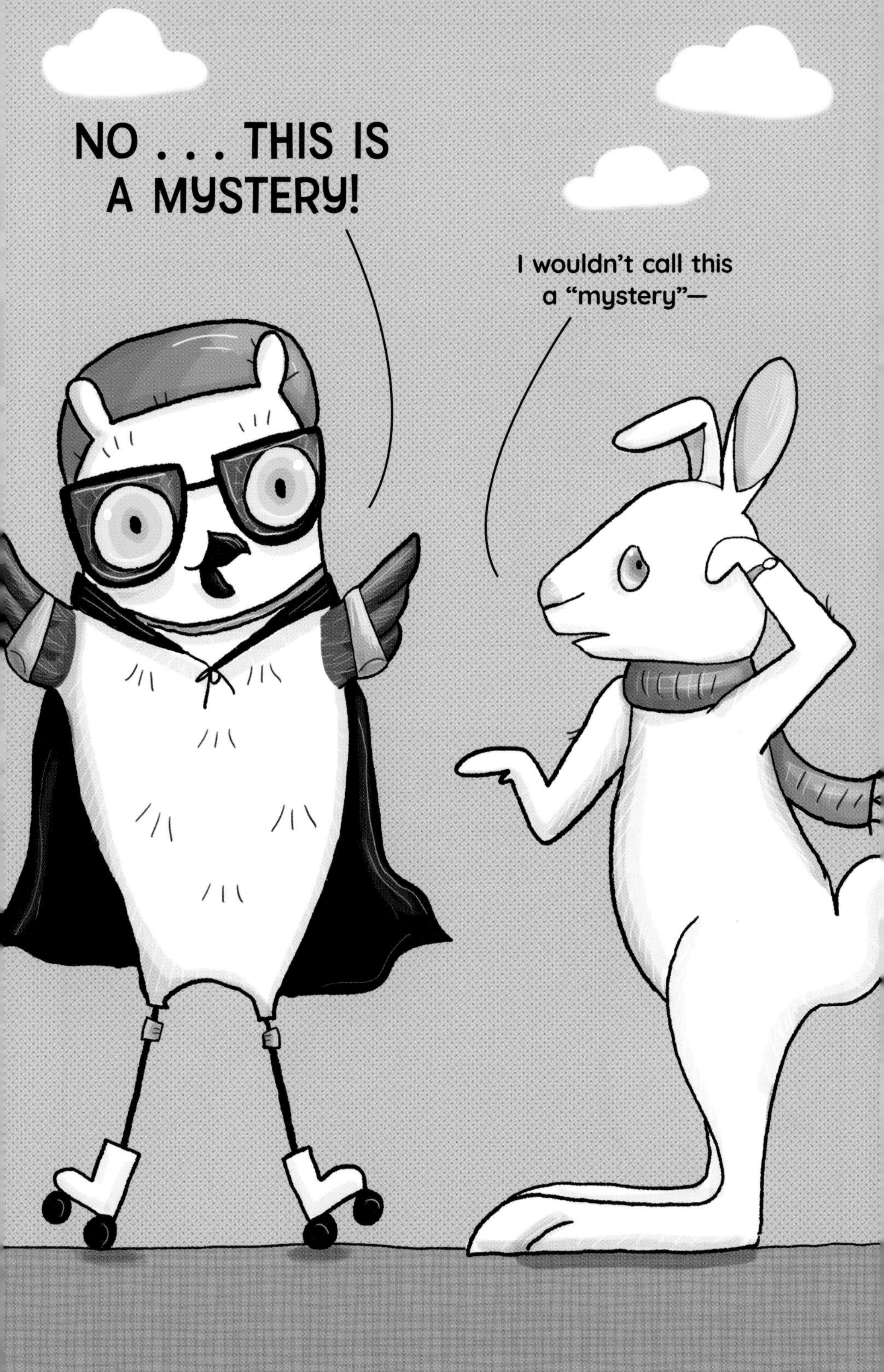
NO . . . THIS IS A MYSTERY!
I wouldn't call this a "mystery"—

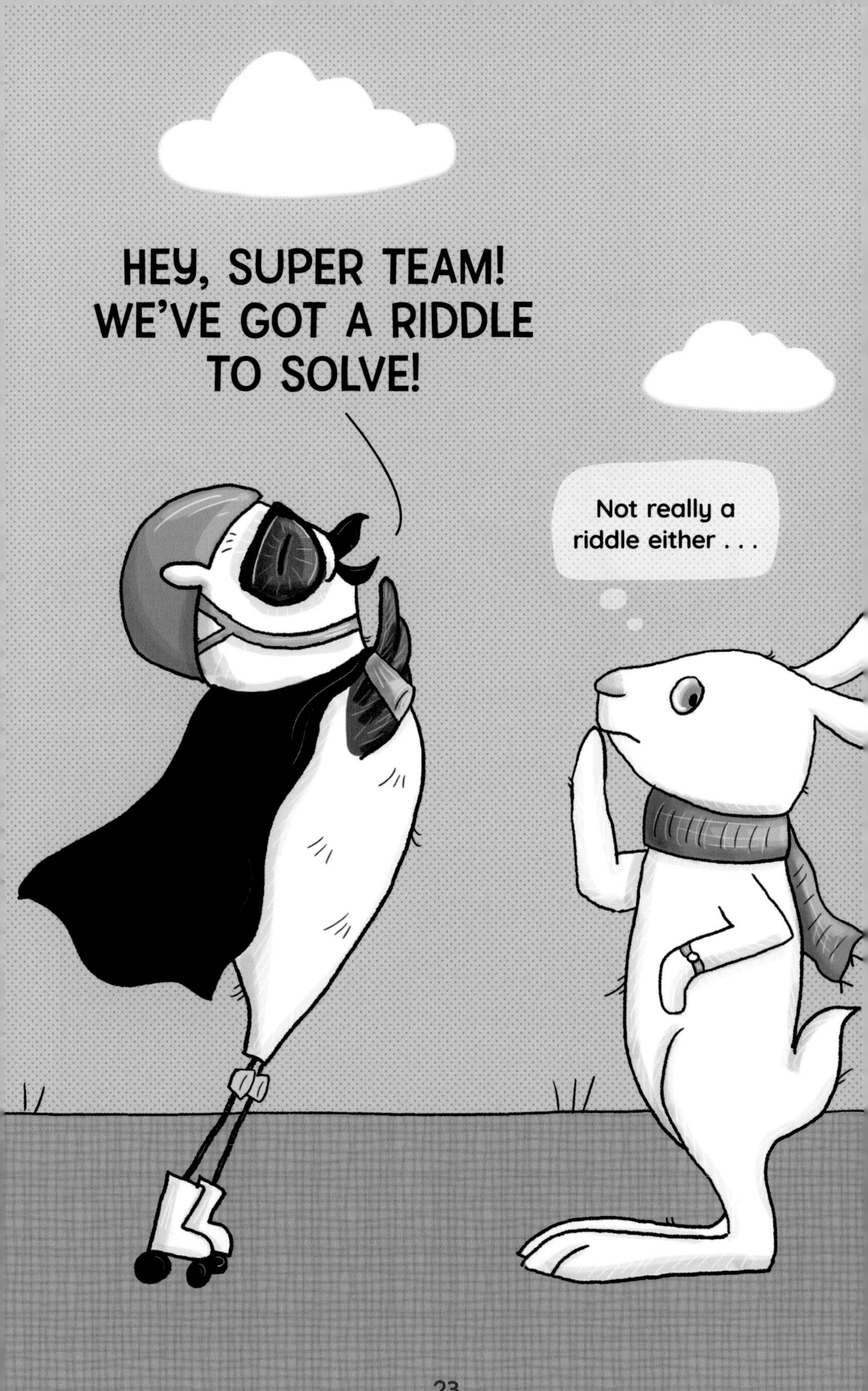
HEY, SUPER TEAM! WE'VE GOT A RIDDLE TO SOLVE!
Not really a riddle either . . .

CHAPTER 3
MY *DEER* FRIENDS

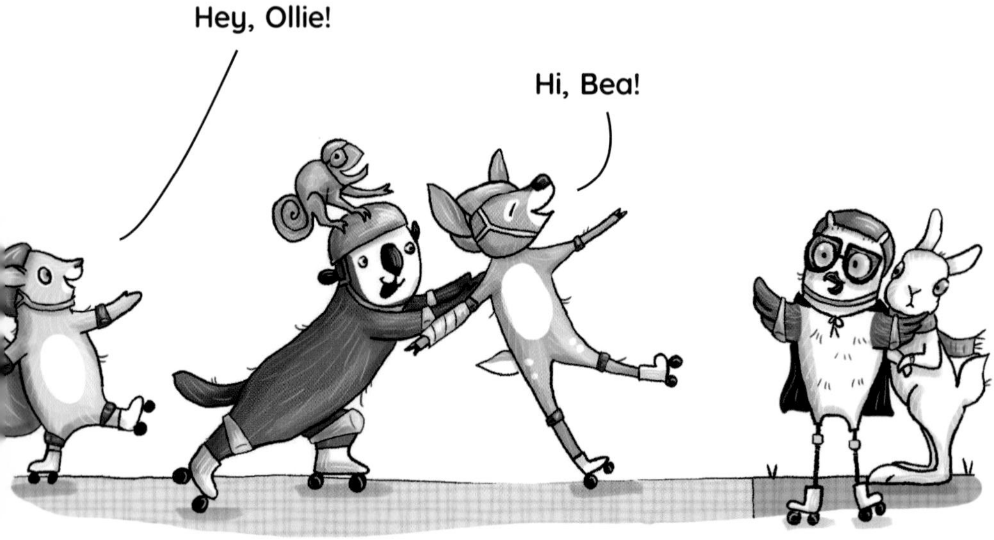
Hey, Ollie!
Hi, Bea!

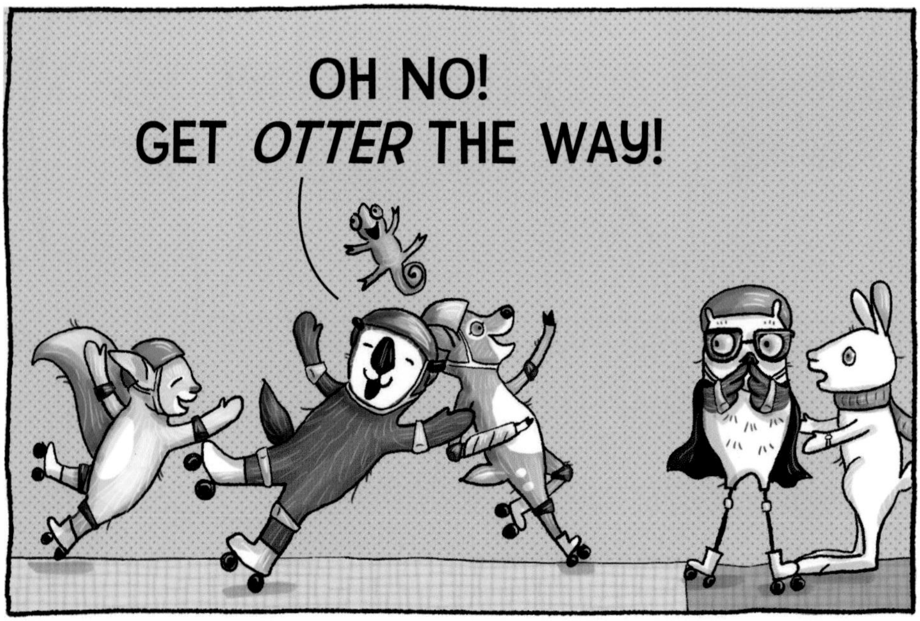
OH NO!
GET *OTTER* THE WAY!

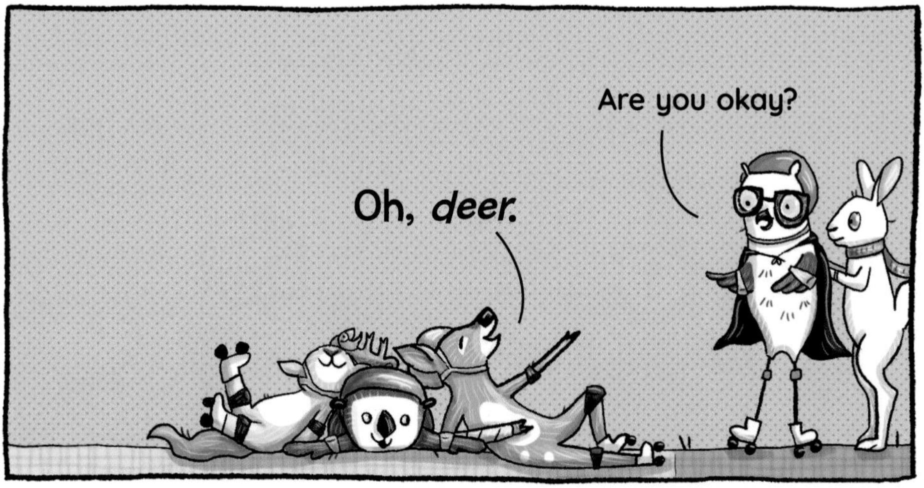
Are you okay?
Oh, *deer.*

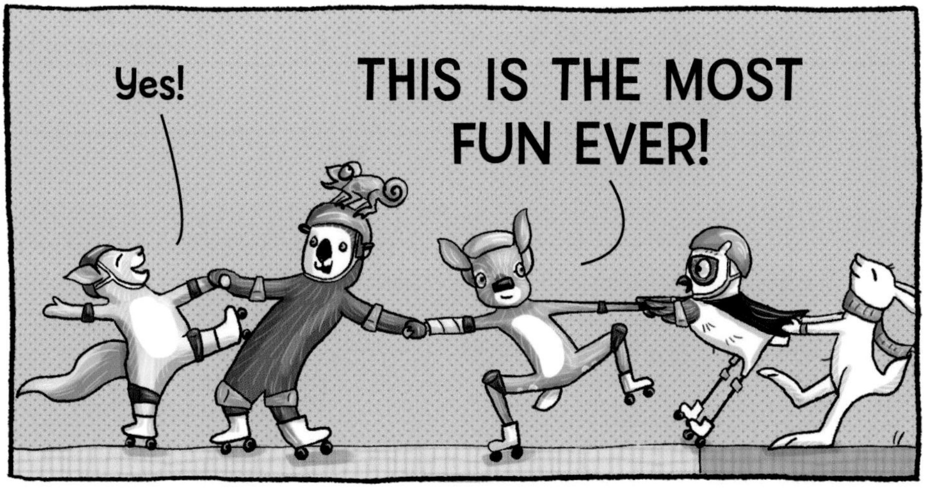
Yes!
THIS IS THE MOST FUN EVER!

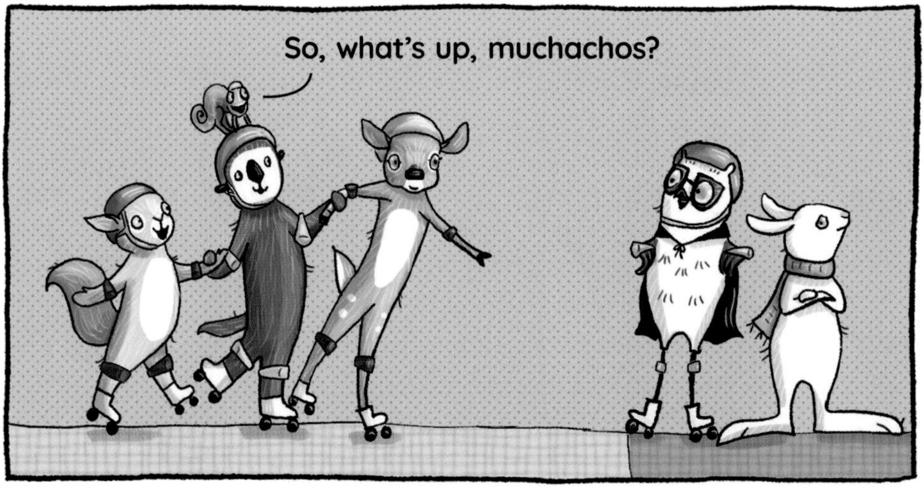
So, what's up, muchachos?

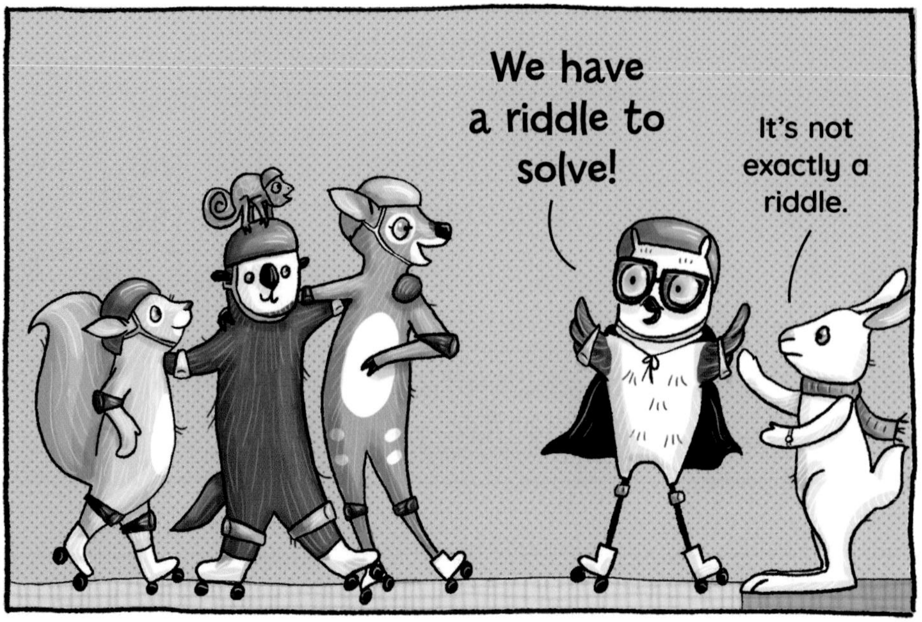
We have a riddle to solve!
It's not exactly a riddle.

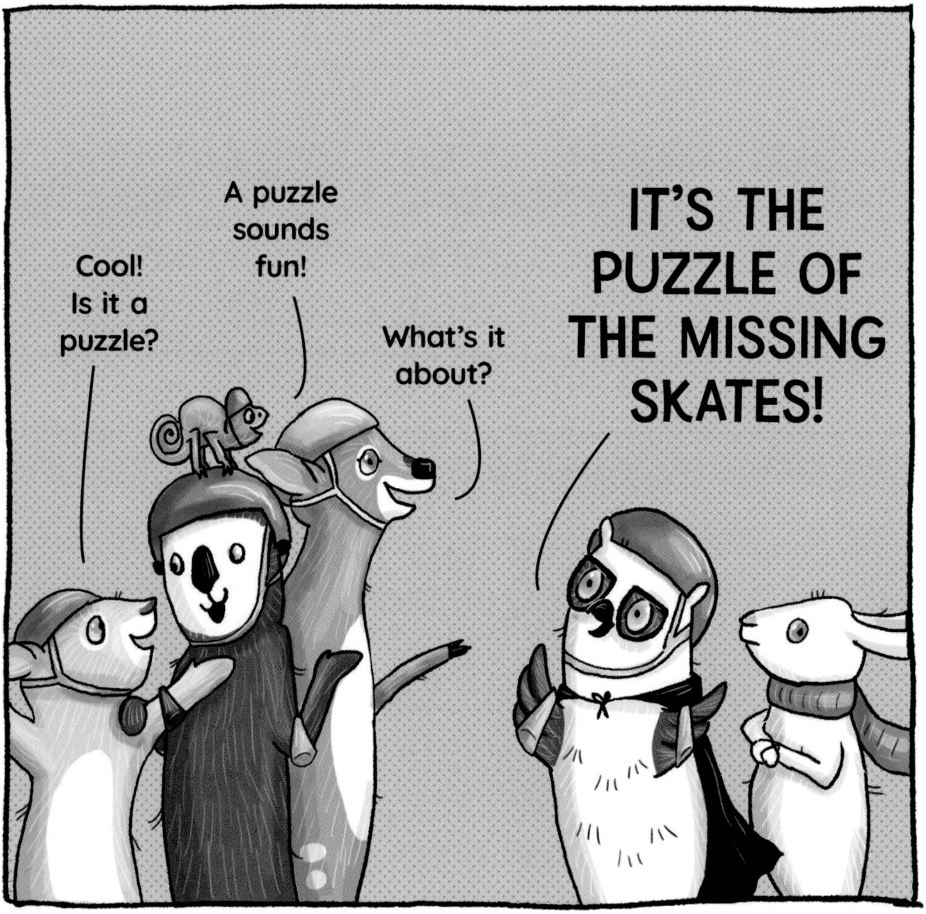
Cool! Is it a puzzle?
A puzzle sounds fun!
What's it about?
IT'S THE PUZZLE OF THE MISSING SKATES!

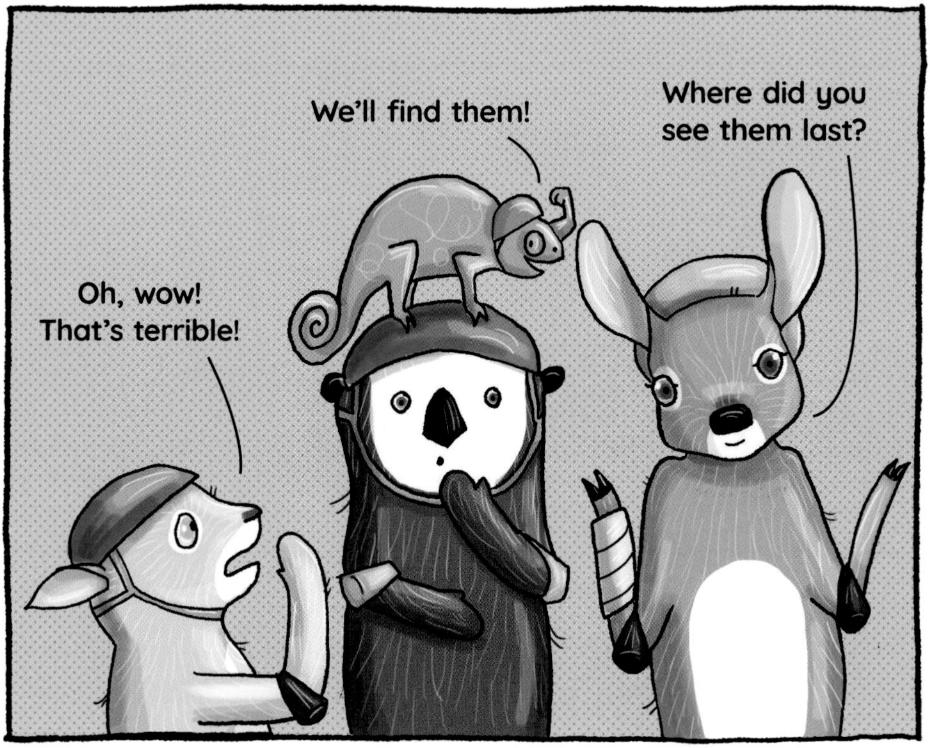
Oh, wow!
That's terrible!
We'll find them!
Where did you
see them last?

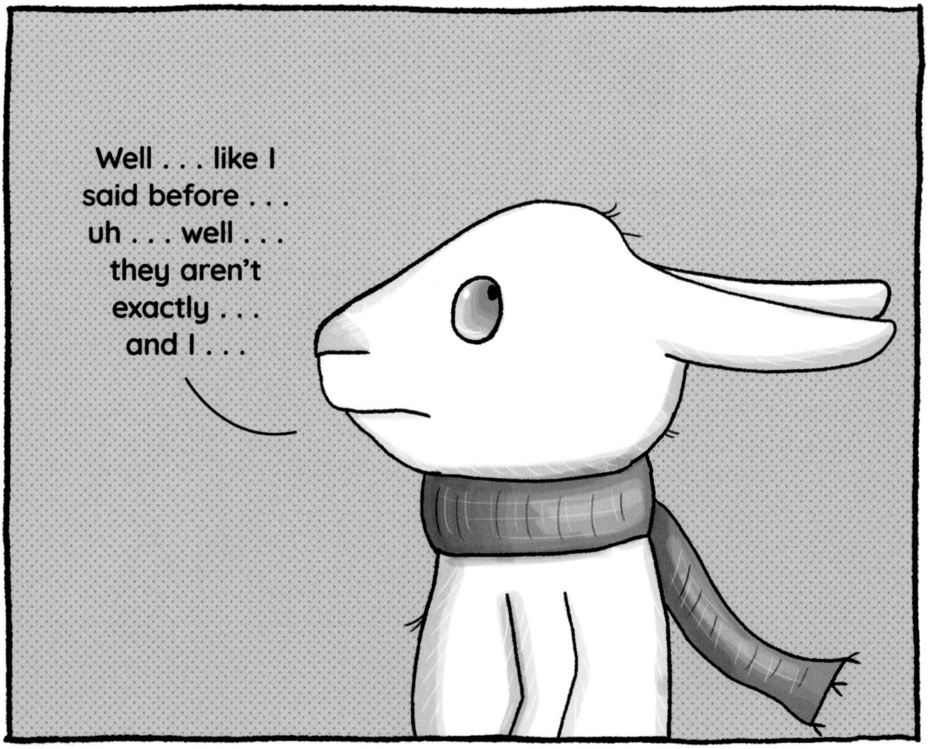
Well . . . like I
said before . . .
uh . . . well . . .
they aren't
exactly . . .
and I . . .

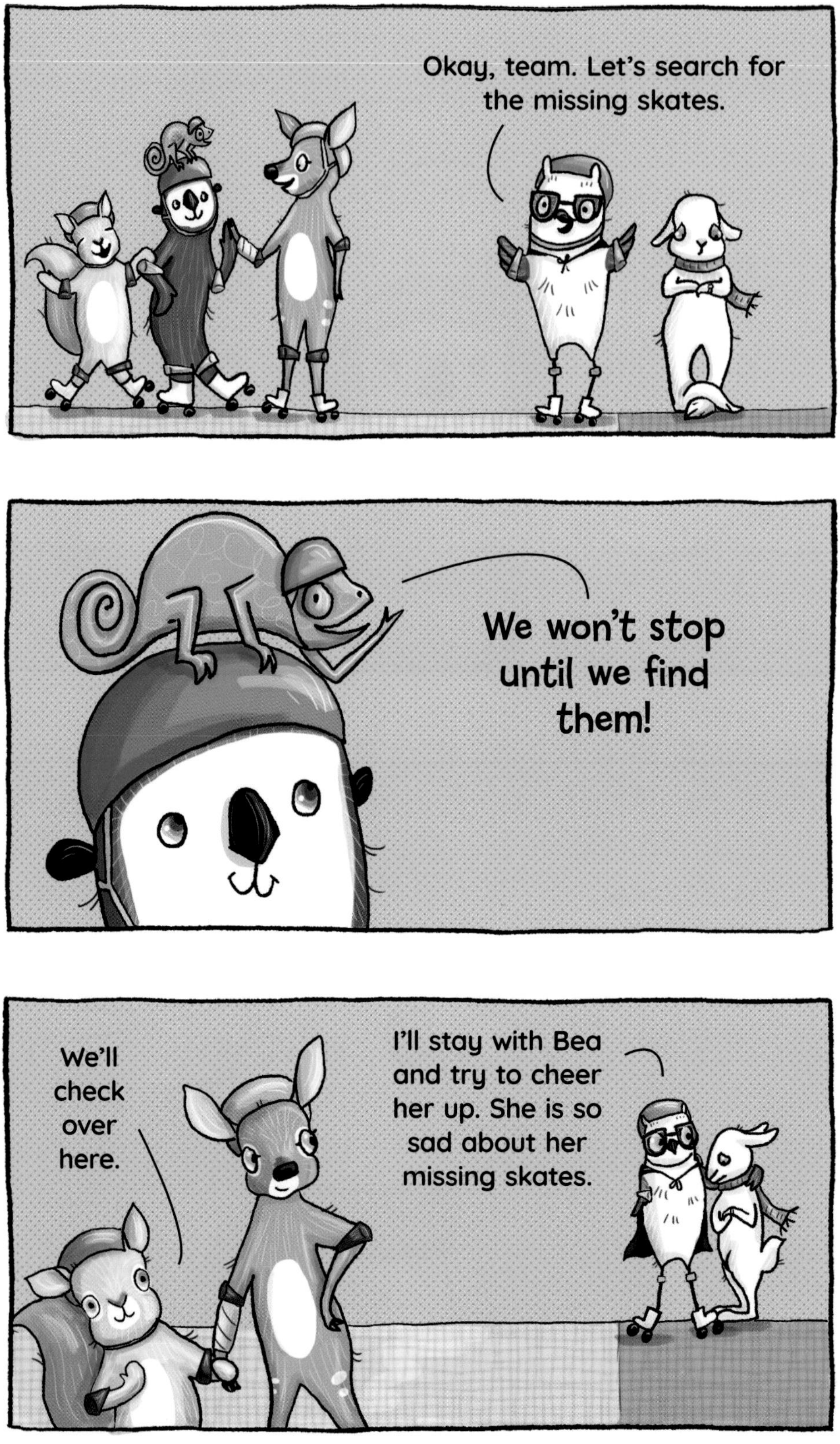
Okay, team. Let's search for the missing skates.
We won't stop until we find them!
We'll check over here.
I'll stay with Bea and try to cheer her up. She is so sad about her missing skates.

WAIT!

EVERYONE COME
BACK!

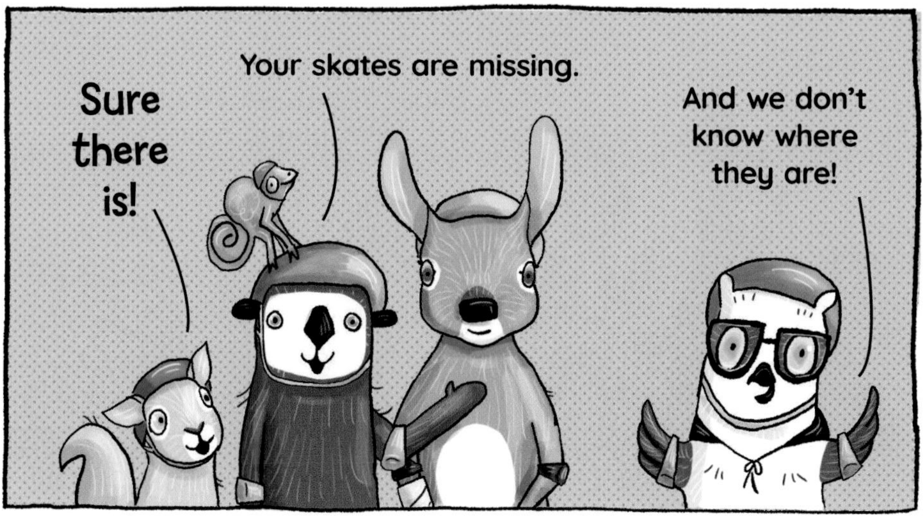
Sure there is!
Your skates are missing.
And we don't know where they are!

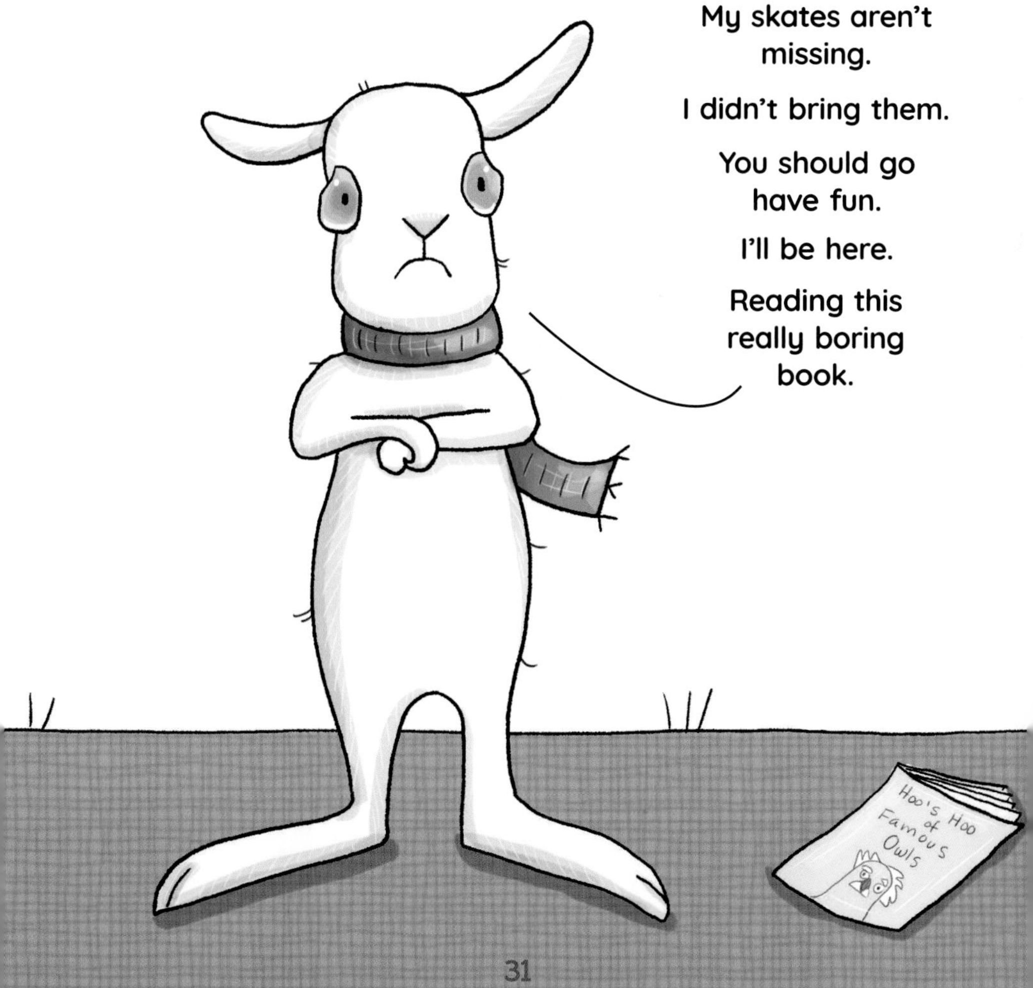
My skates aren't missing.
I didn't bring them.
You should go have fun.
I'll be here.
Reading this really boring book.
Hoo's Hoo of Famous Owls

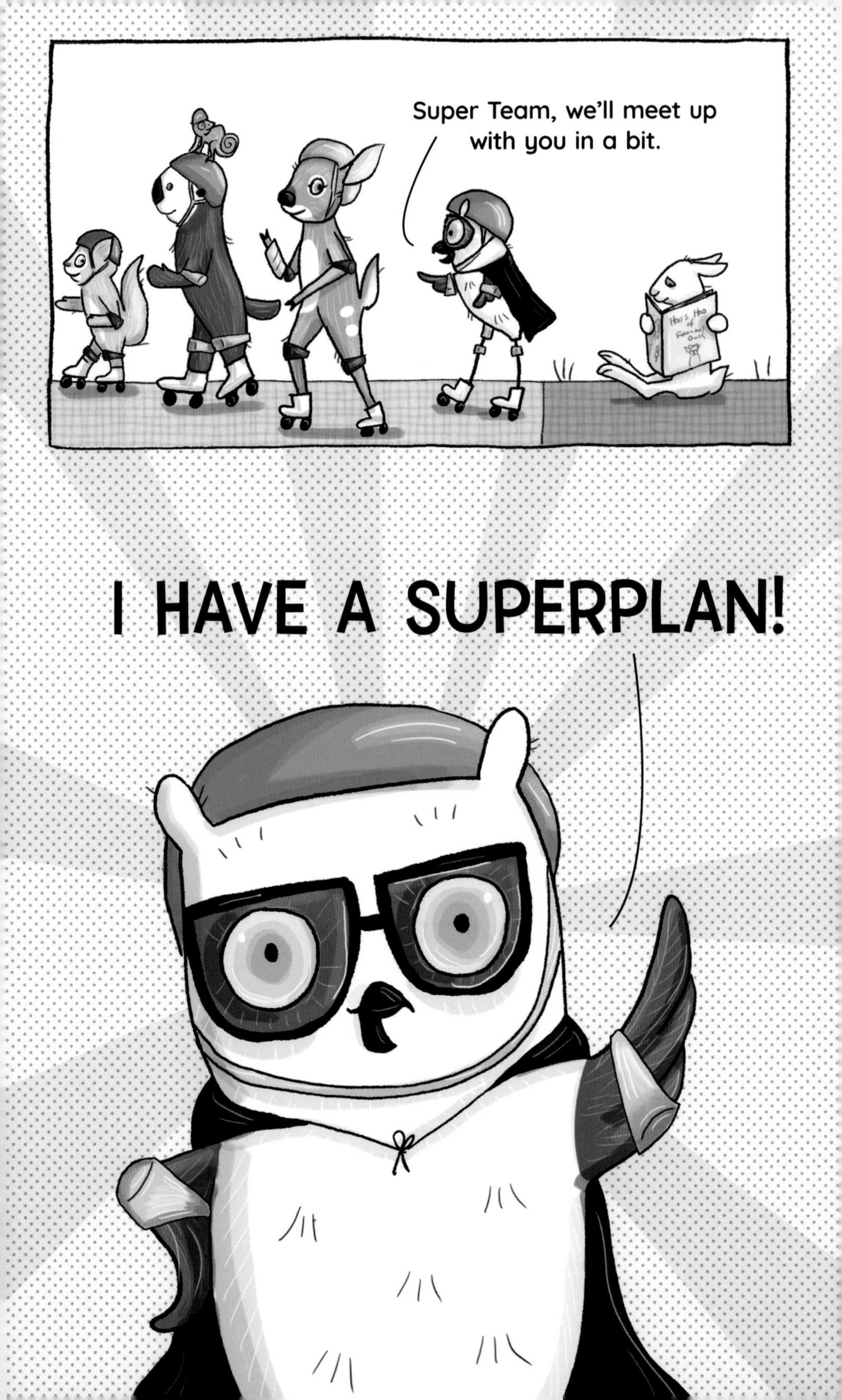
Super Team, we'll meet up with you in a bit.
I HAVE A SUPERPLAN!

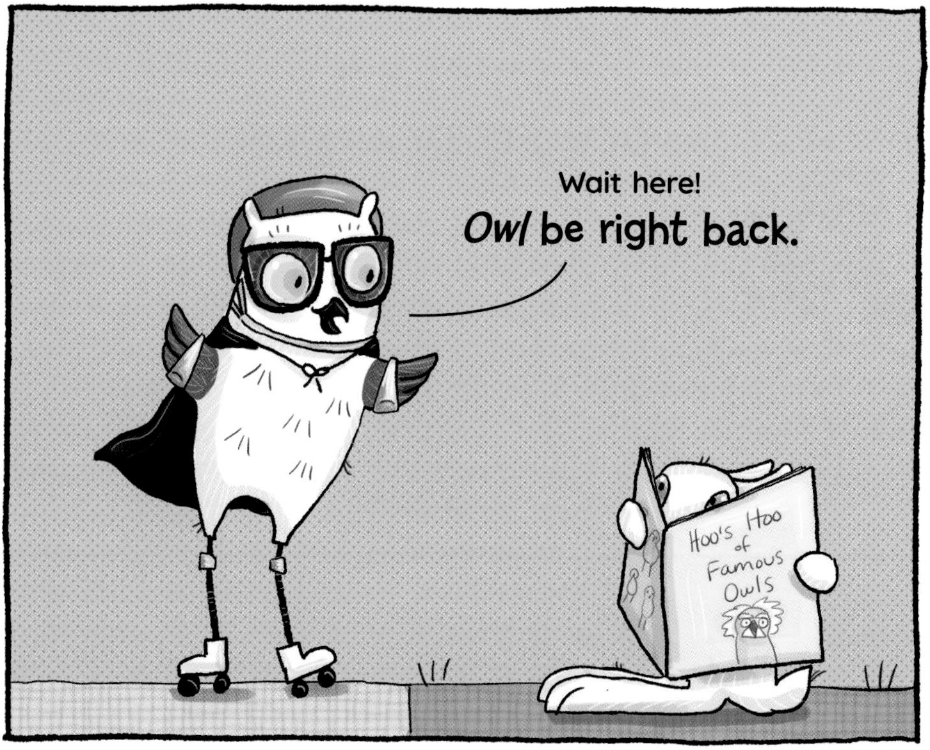
Wait here!
Owl be right back.
Hoo's Hoo of Famous Owls

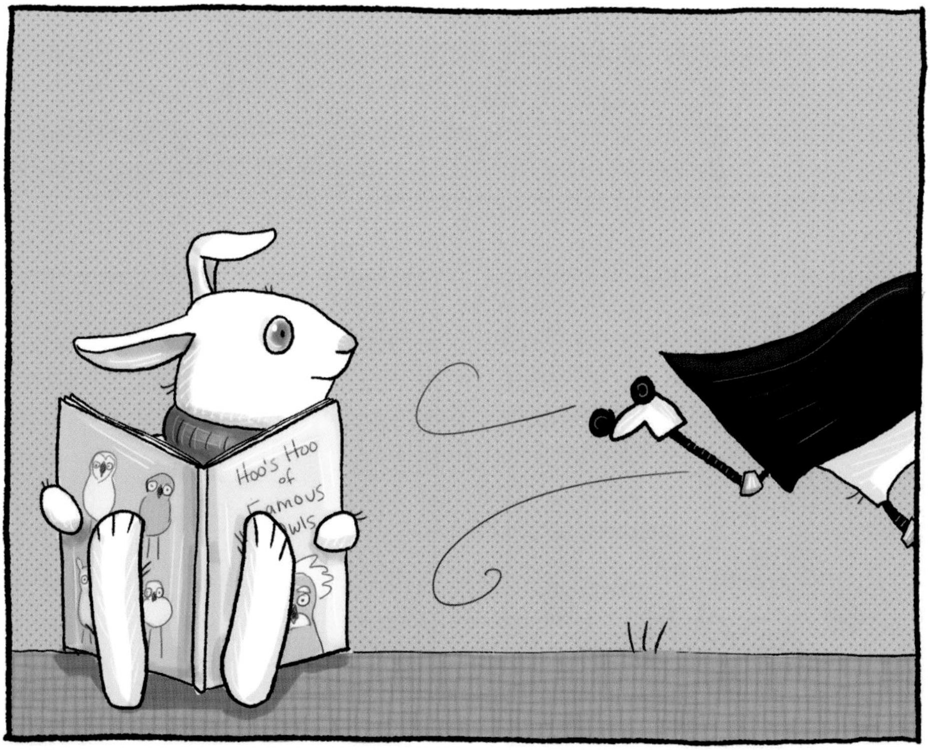
Hoo's Hoo of Famous Owls

CHAPTER 4

POLAR ROLLERS

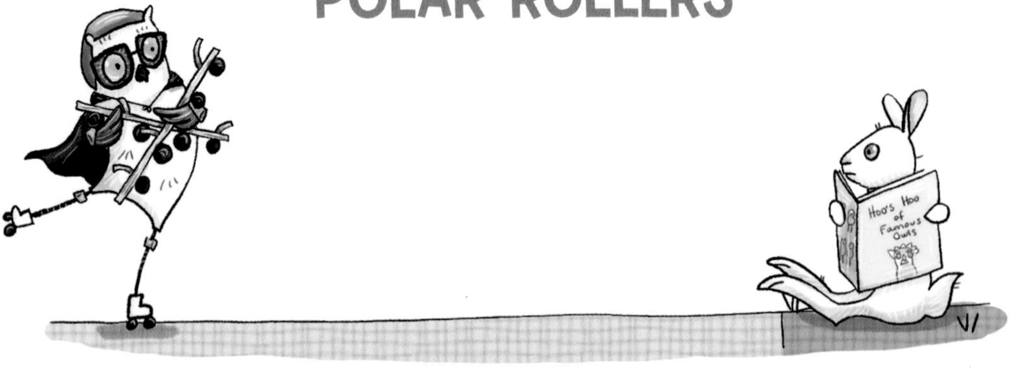
Hoo's Hoo of Famous Owls

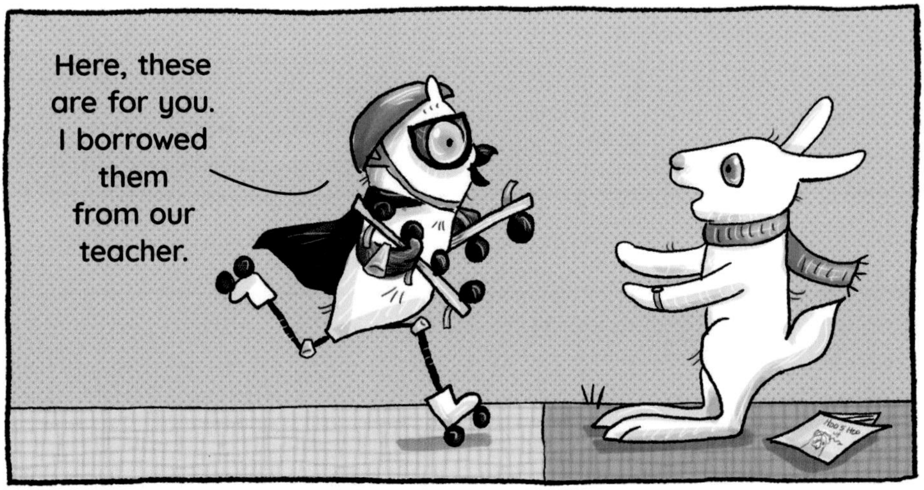
Here, these are for you. I borrowed them from our teacher.

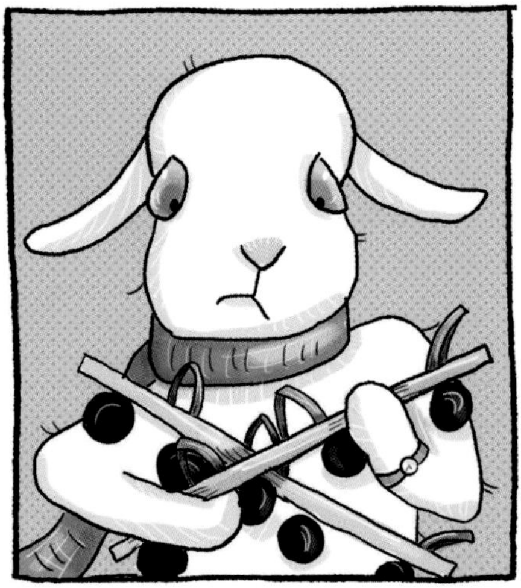

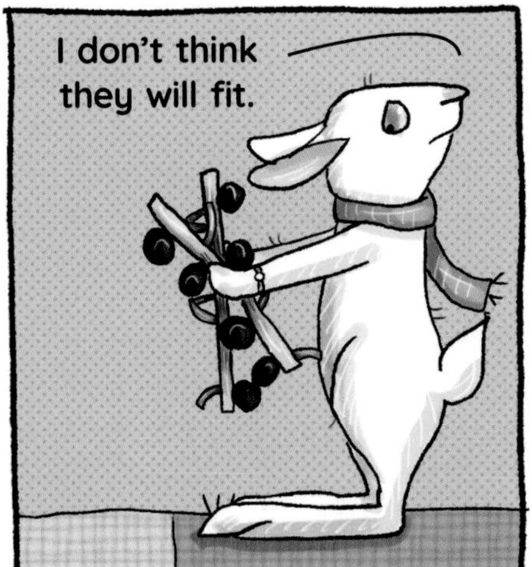
I don't think they will fit.

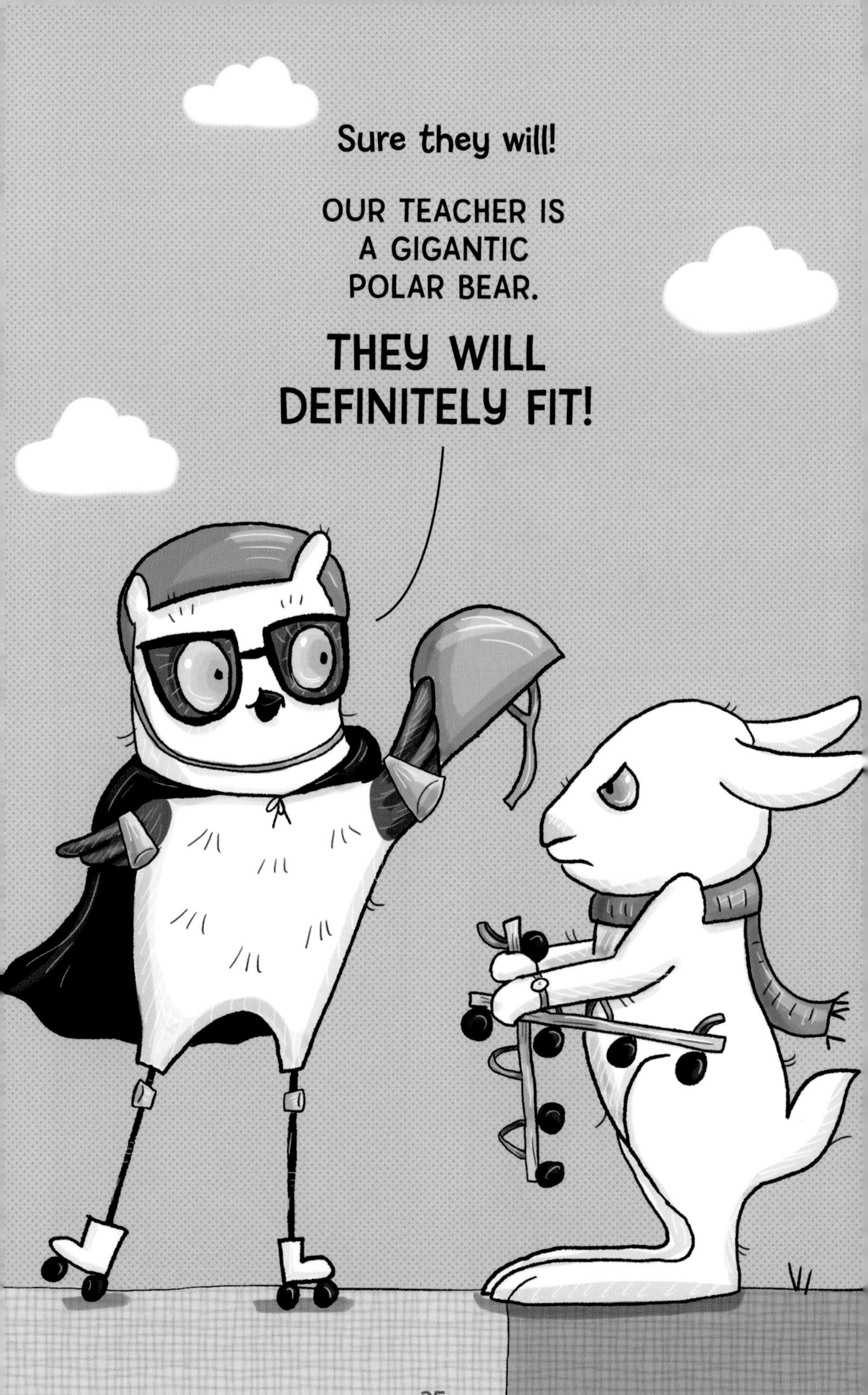
Sure they will!
OUR TEACHER IS A GIGANTIC POLAR BEAR.
THEY WILL DEFINITELY FIT!

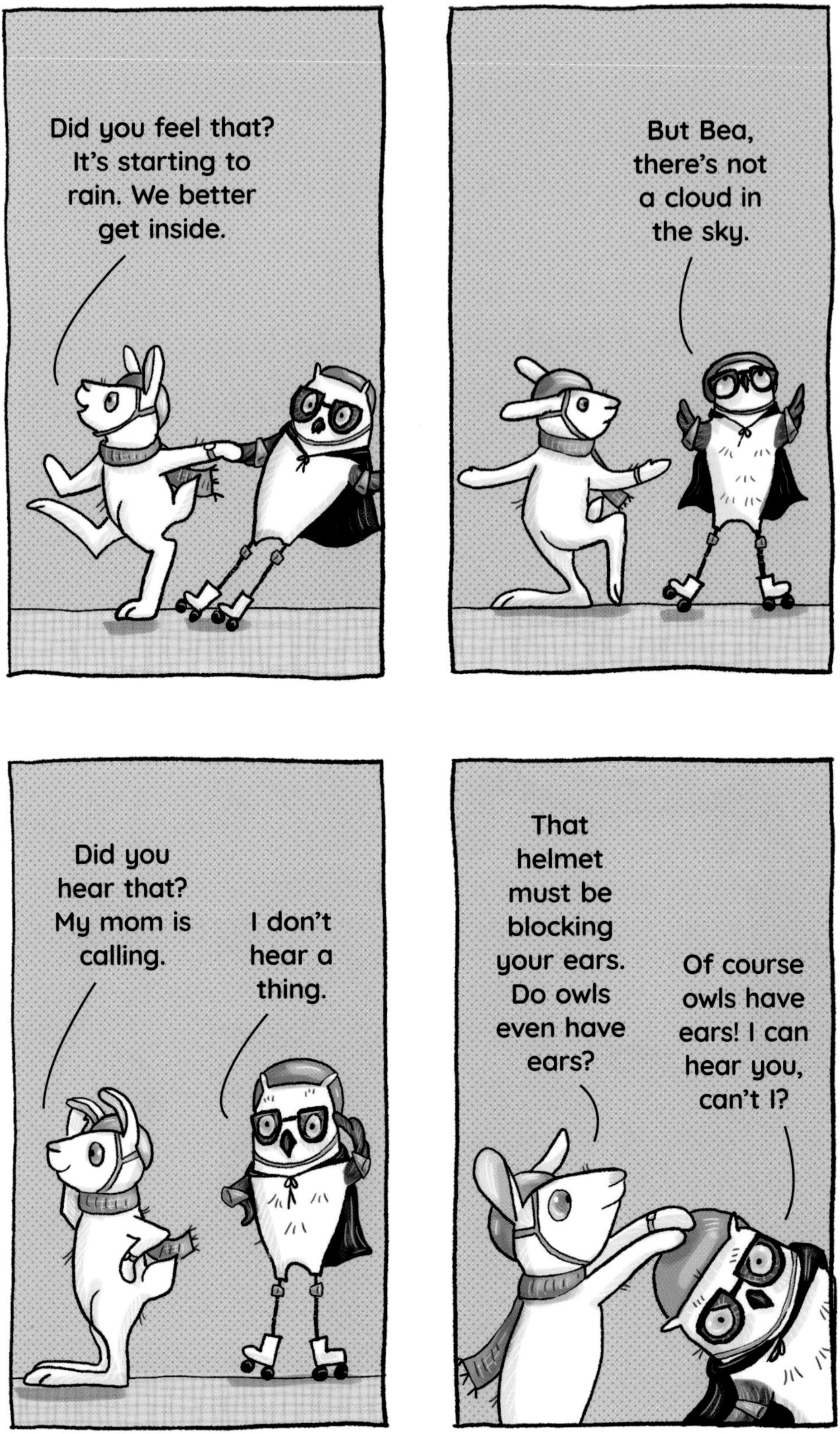
Did you feel that? It's starting to rain. We better get inside.
But Bea, there's not a cloud in the sky.
Did you hear that? My mom is calling.
I don't hear a thing.
That helmet must be blocking your ears. Do owls even have ears?
Of course owls have ears! I can hear you, can't I?

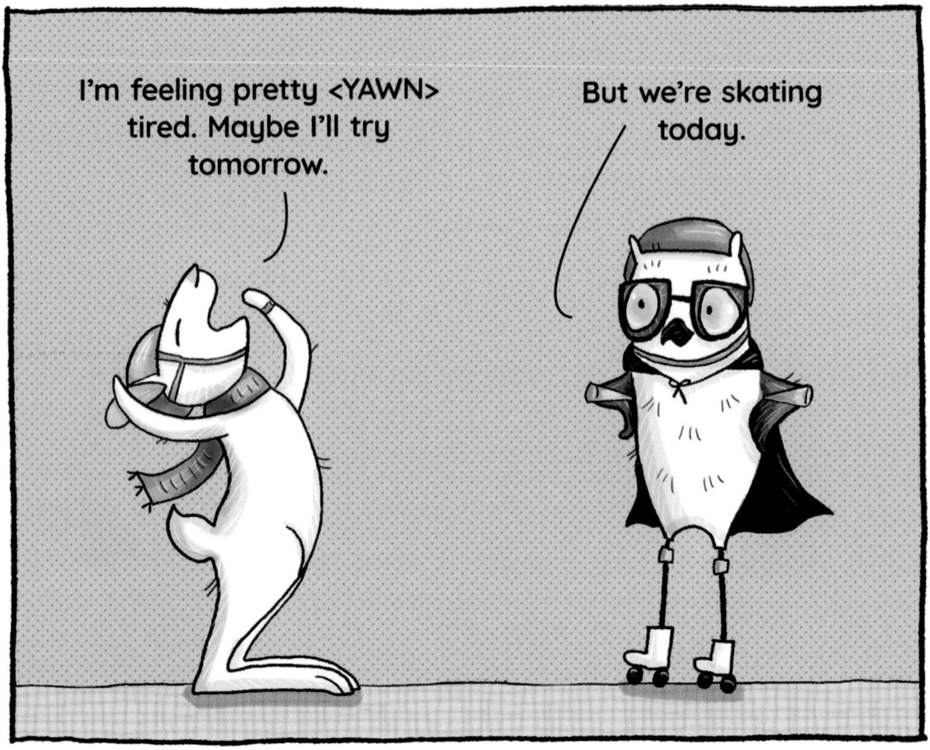
I'm feeling pretty <YAWN> tired. Maybe I'll try tomorrow.
But we're skating today.

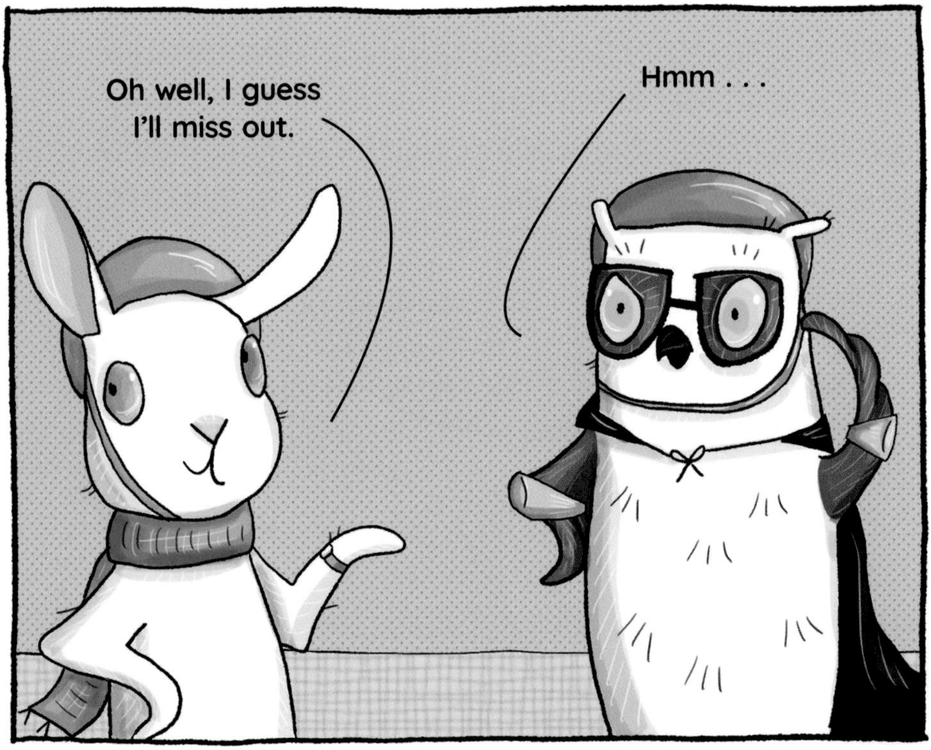
Oh well, I guess I'll miss out.
Hmm . . .

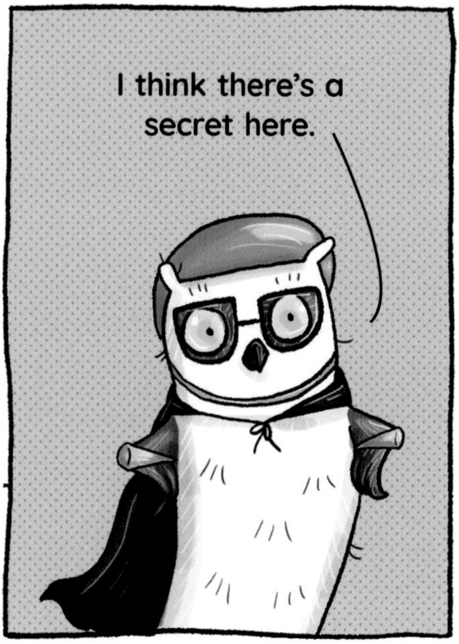
I think there's a secret here.

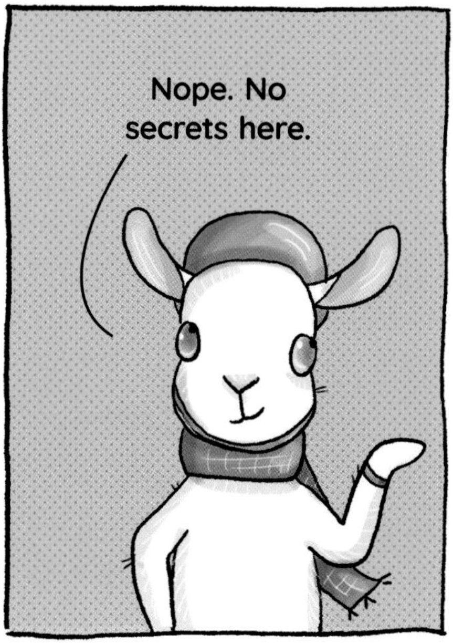
Nope. No secrets here.

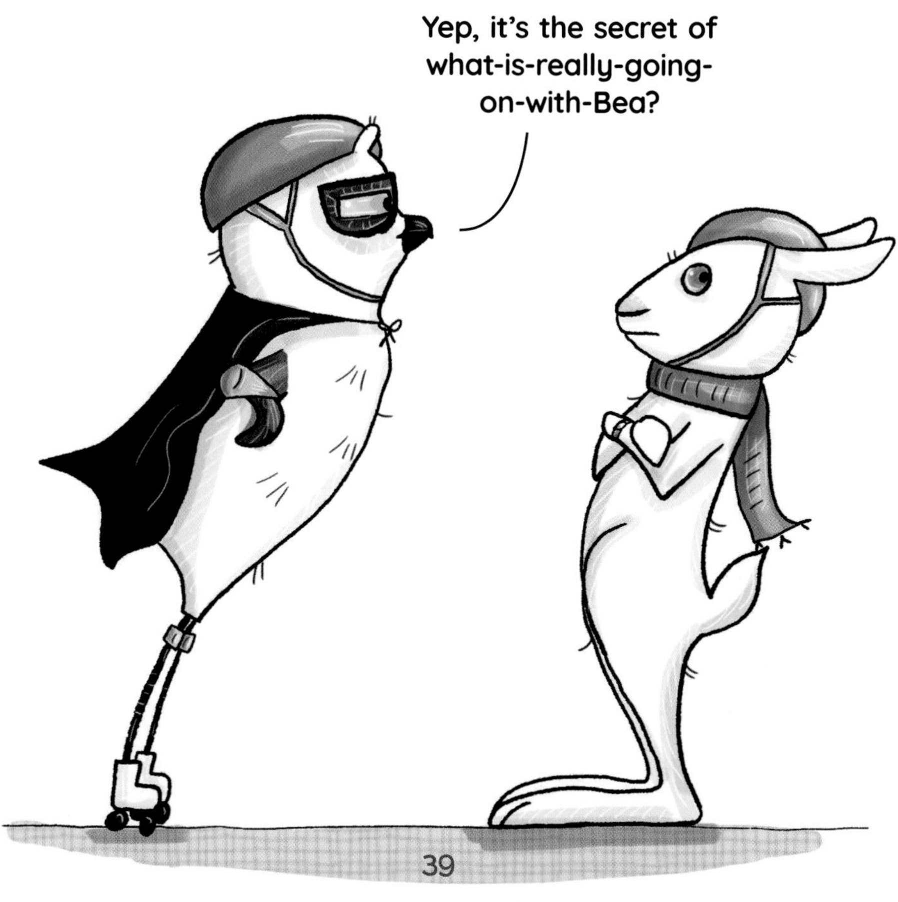
Yep, it's the secret of what-is-really-going-on-with-Bea?

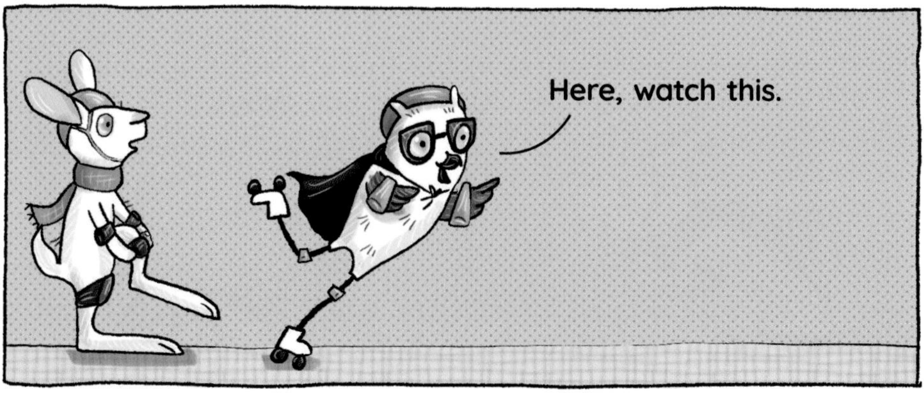
Here, watch this.

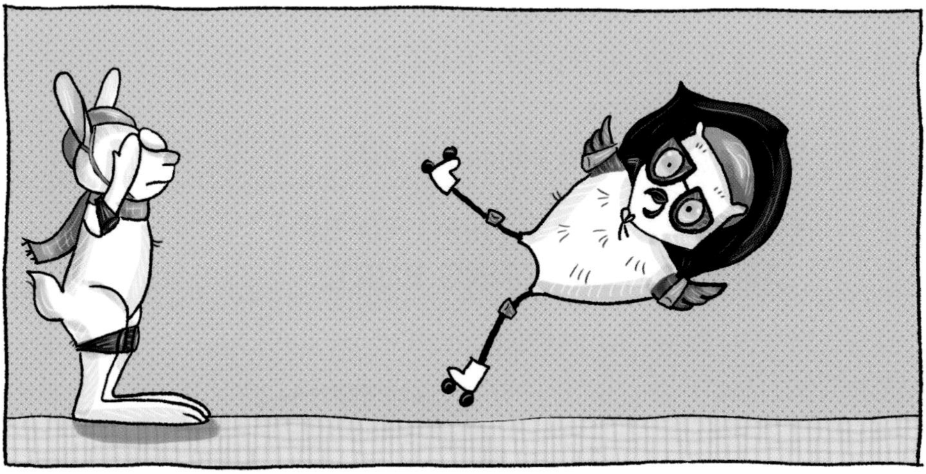

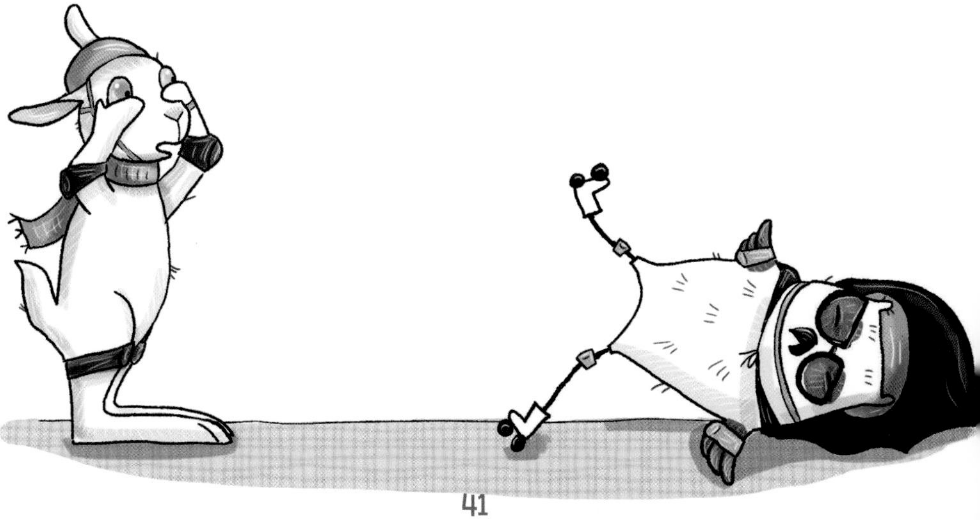

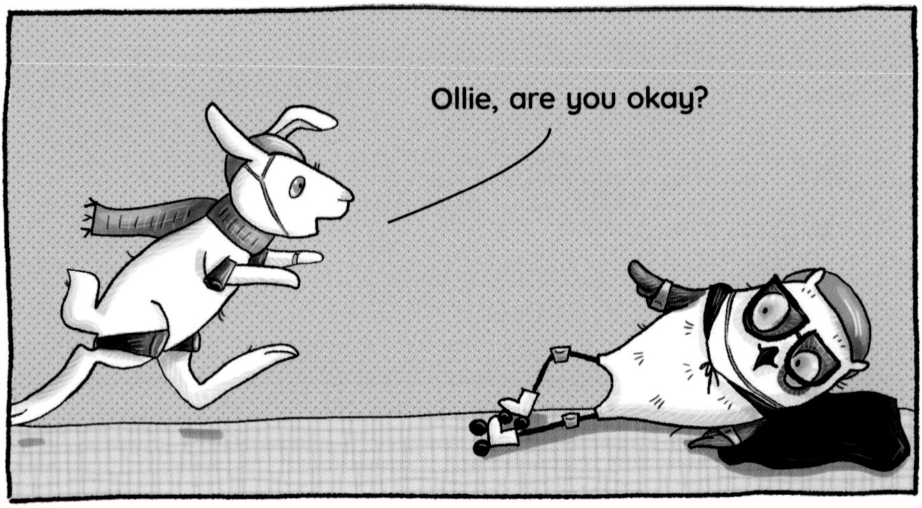
Ollie, are you okay?

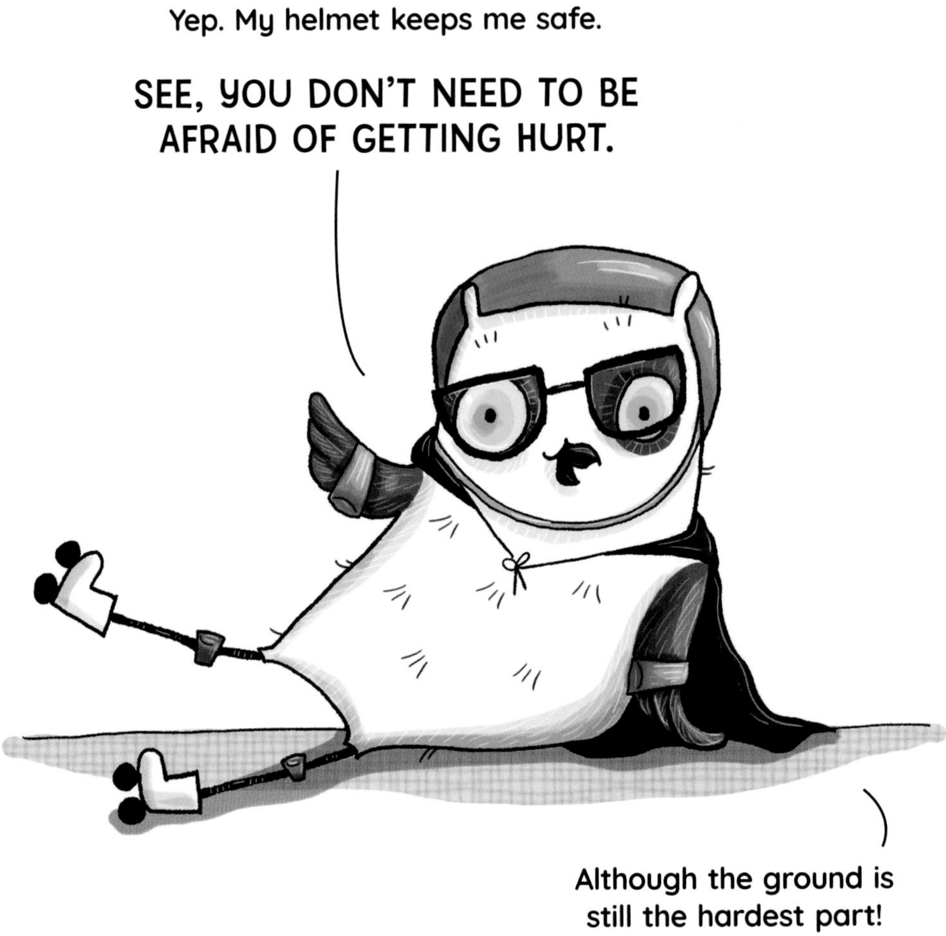
Yep. My helmet keeps me safe.
SEE, YOU DON'T NEED TO BE AFRAID OF GETTING HURT.
Although the ground is still the hardest part!

43

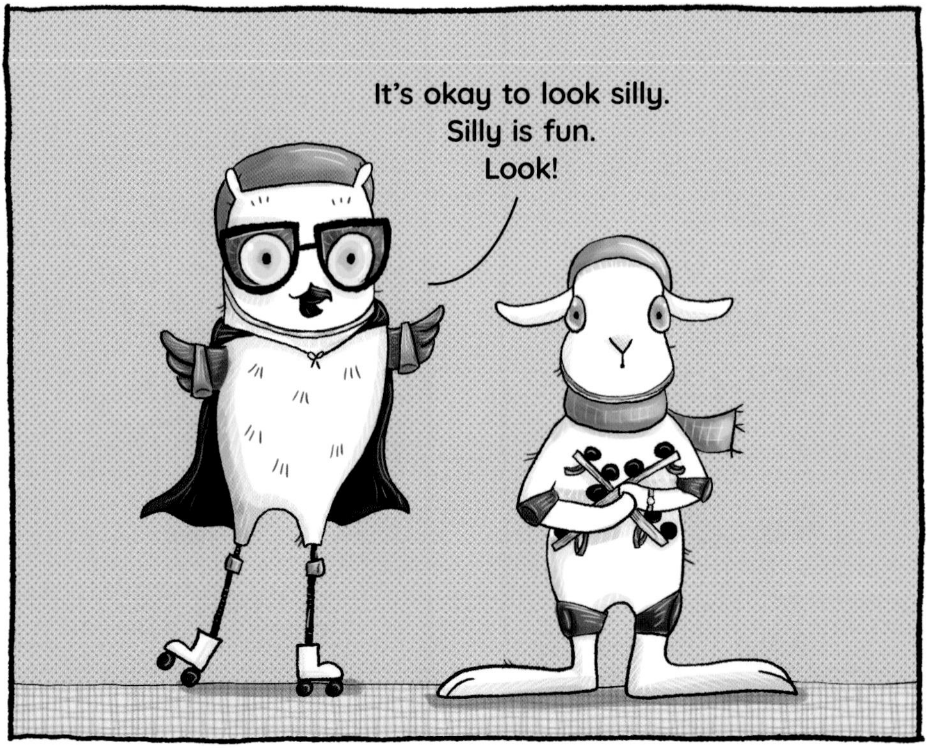
It's okay to look silly.
Silly is fun.
Look!

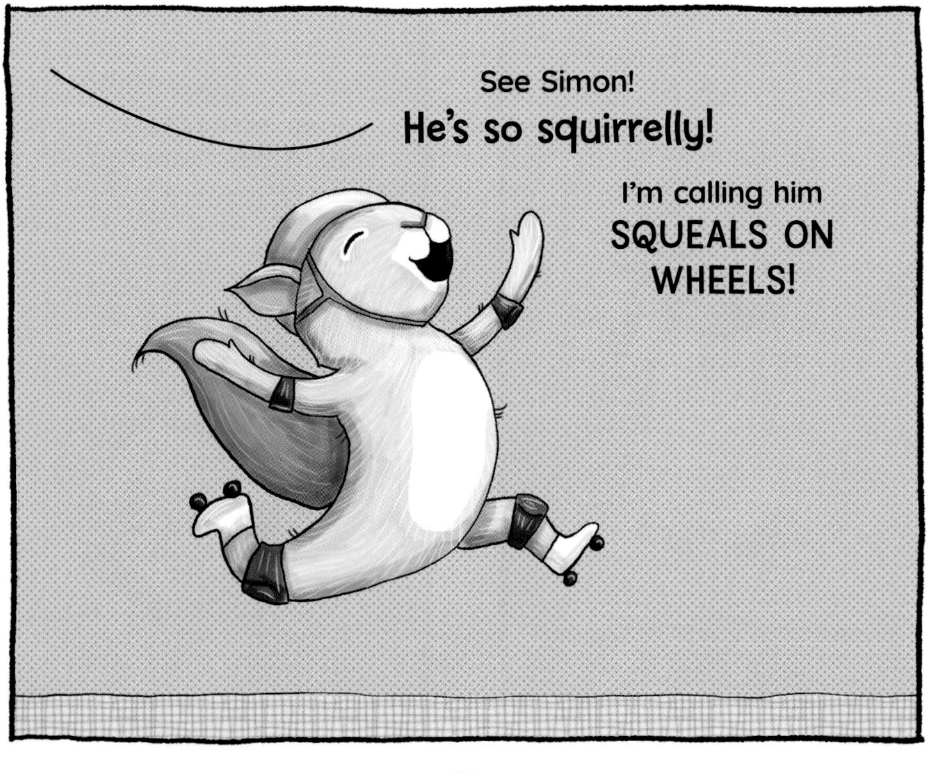
See Simon!
He's so squirrelly!
I'm calling him
SQUEALS ON
WHEELS!

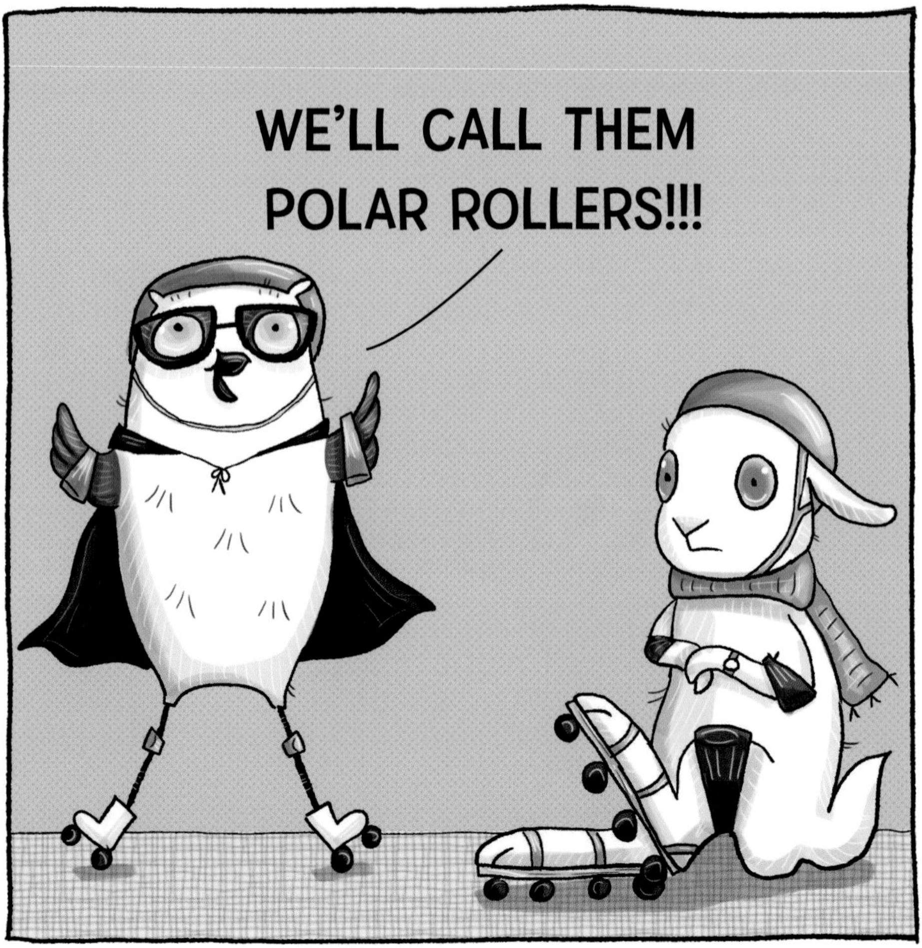
WE'LL CALL THEM
POLAR ROLLERS!!!

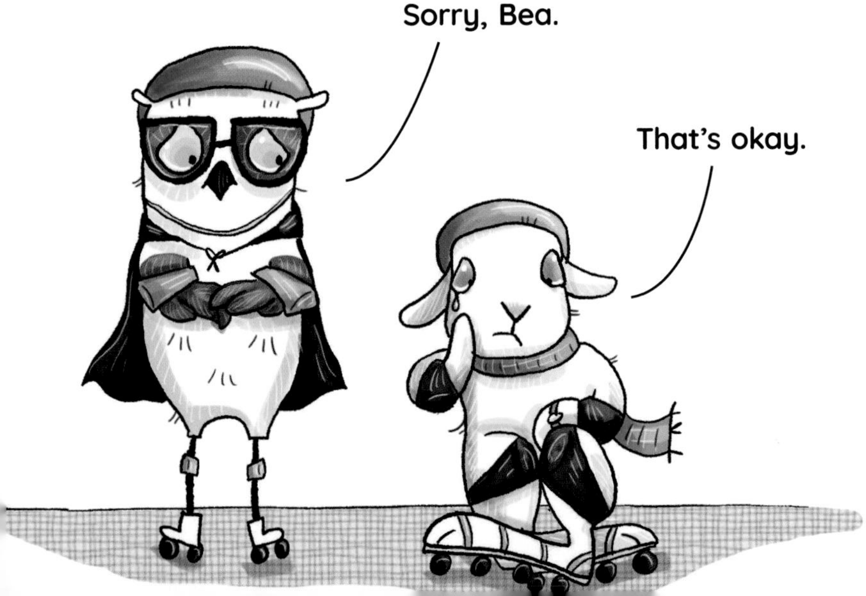
Sorry, Bea.
That's okay.

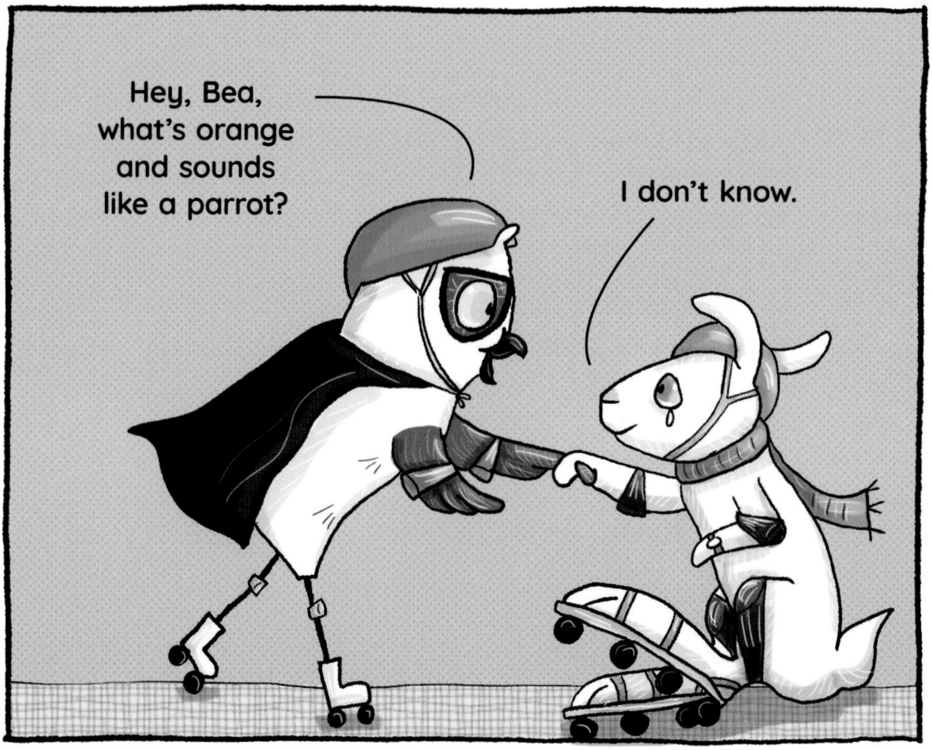
Hey, Bea,
what's orange
and sounds
like a parrot?
I don't know.

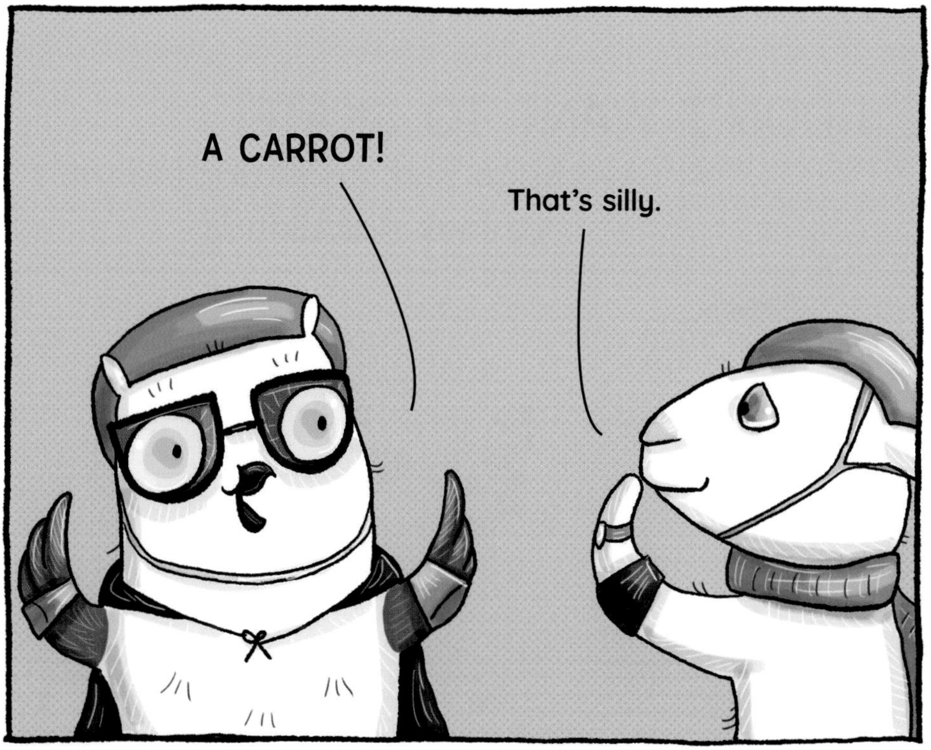
A CARROT!
That's silly.

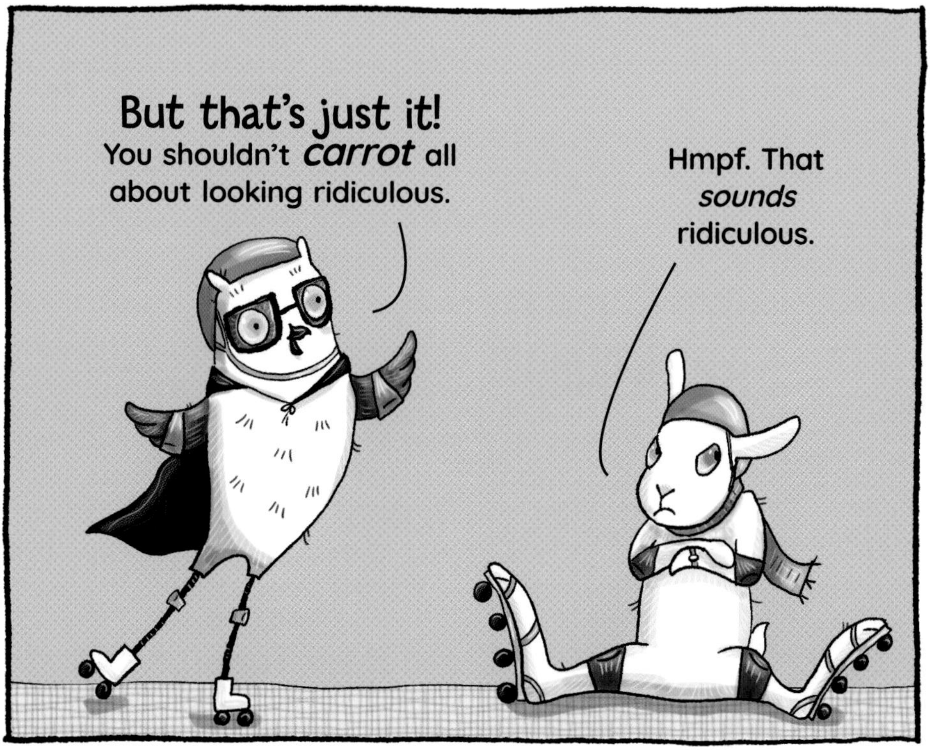
But that's just it!
You shouldn't carrot all about looking ridiculous.
Hmpf. That sounds ridiculous.

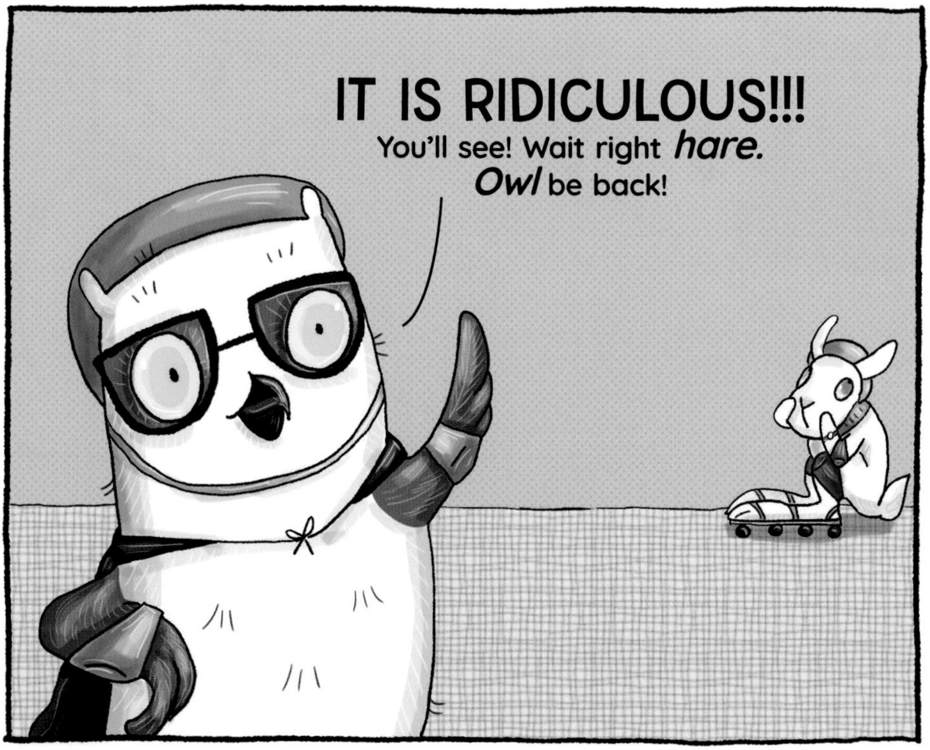
IT IS RIDICULOUS!!!
You'll see! Wait right hare. Owl be back!

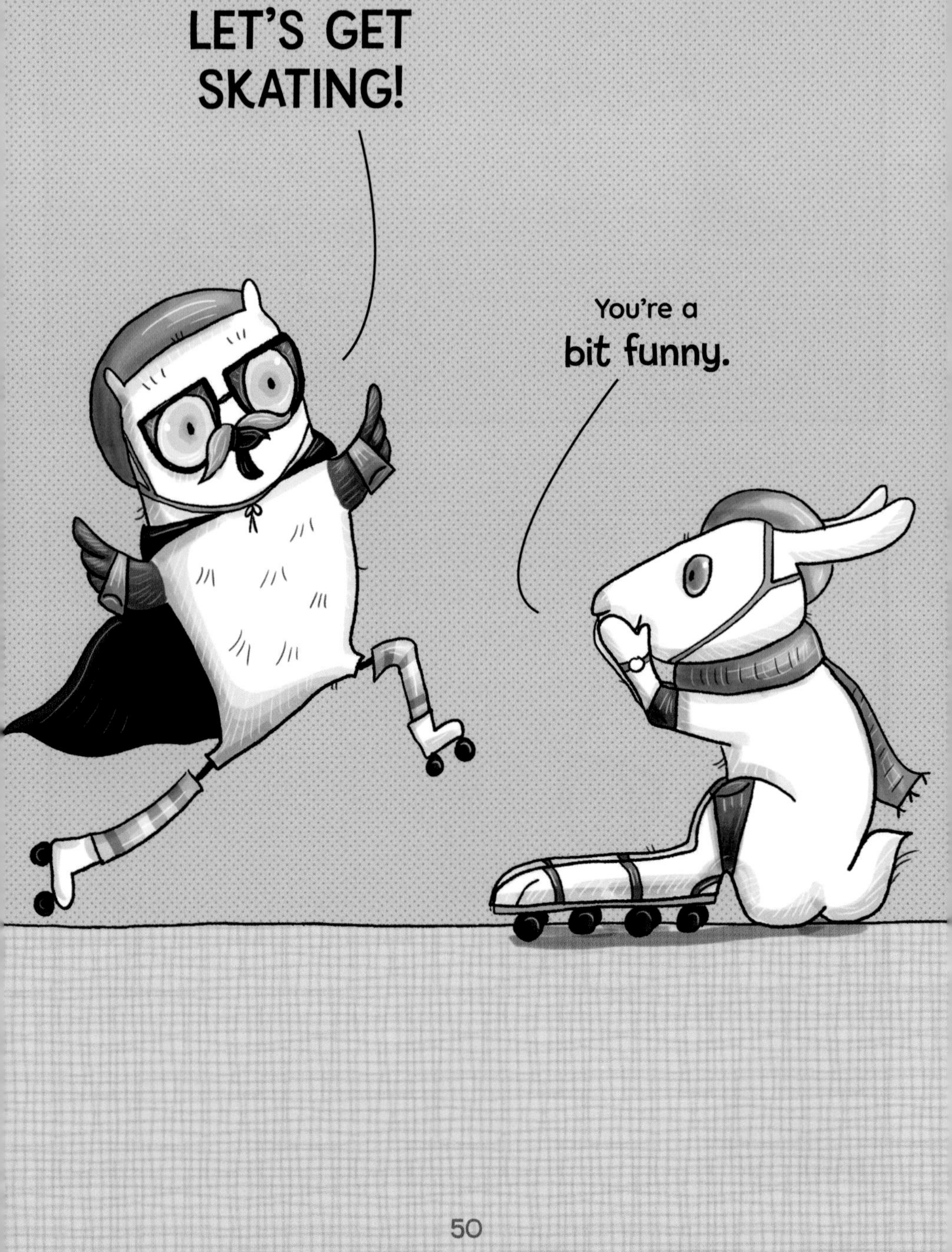
LET'S GET SKATING!
You're a bit funny.

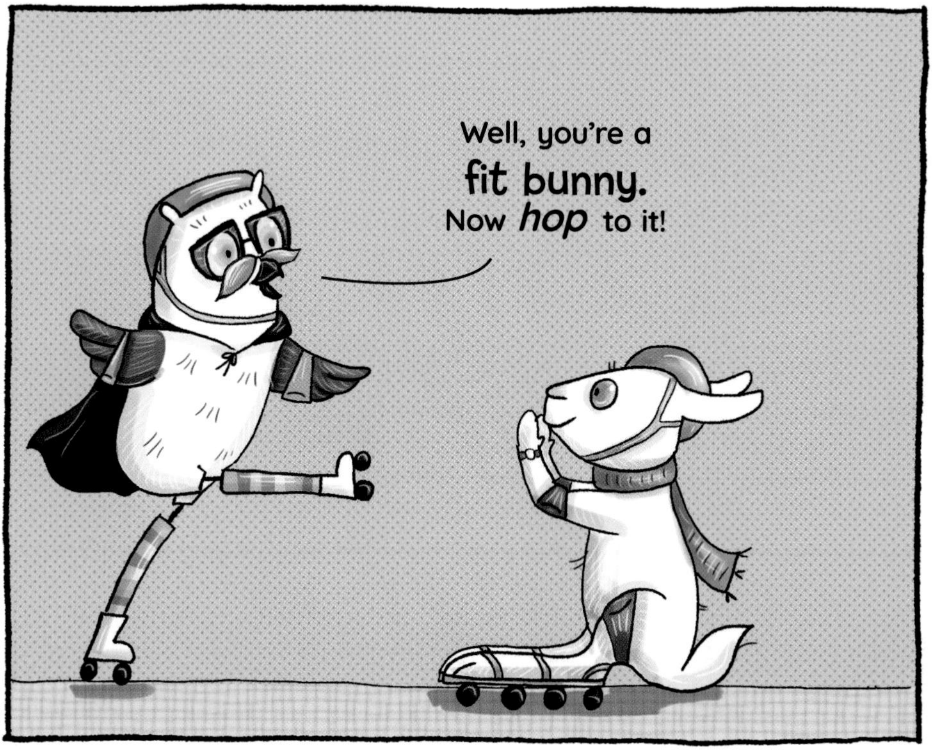
Well, you're a fit bunny. Now hop to it!

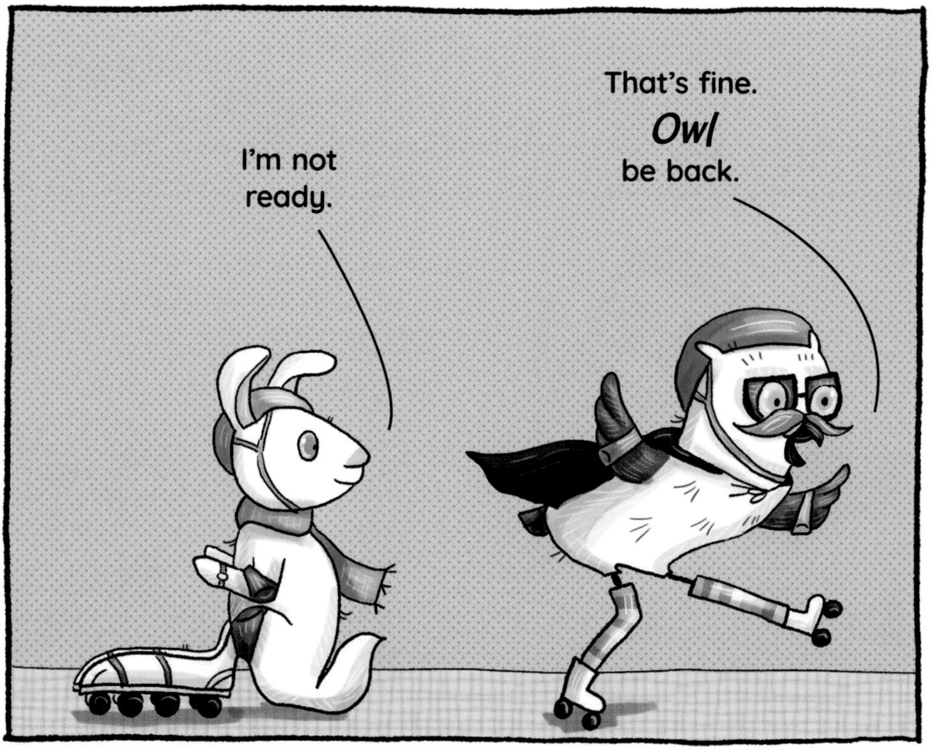
I'm not ready.
That's fine. Owl be back.

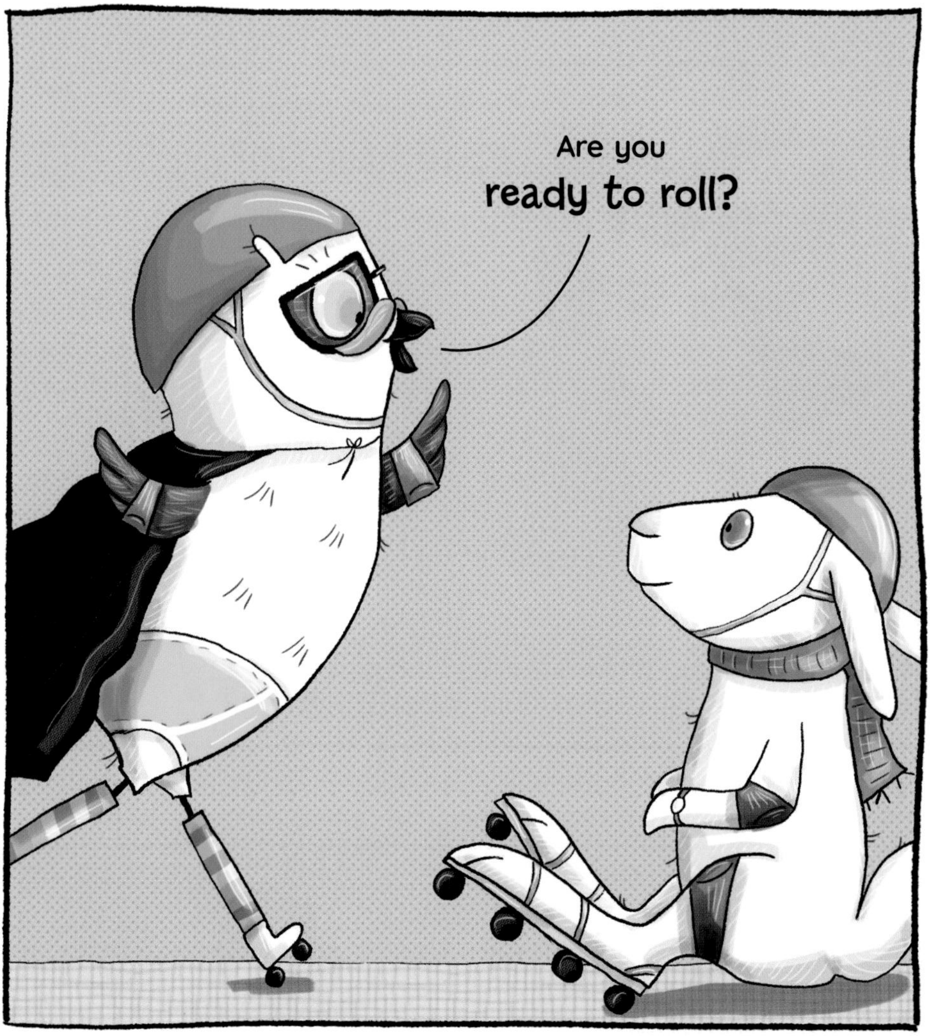
Are you
ready to roll?

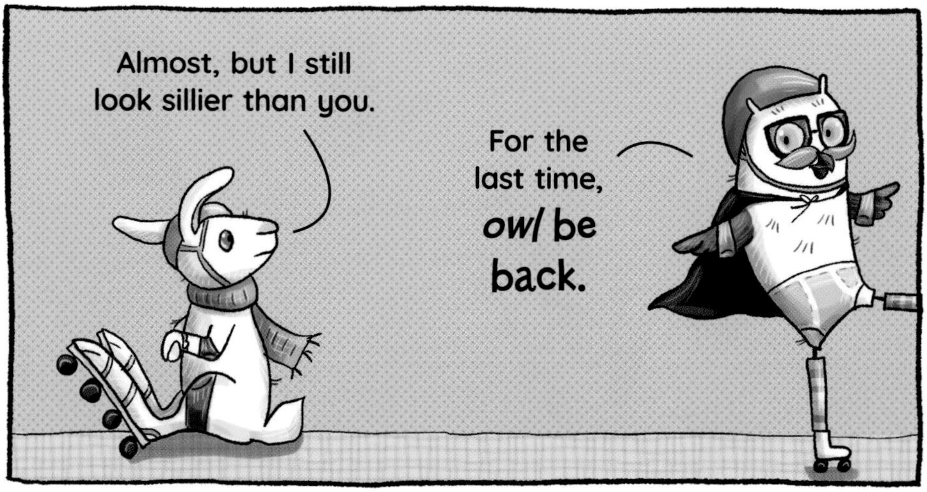
Almost, but I still
look sillier than you.
For the
last time,
owl be
back.

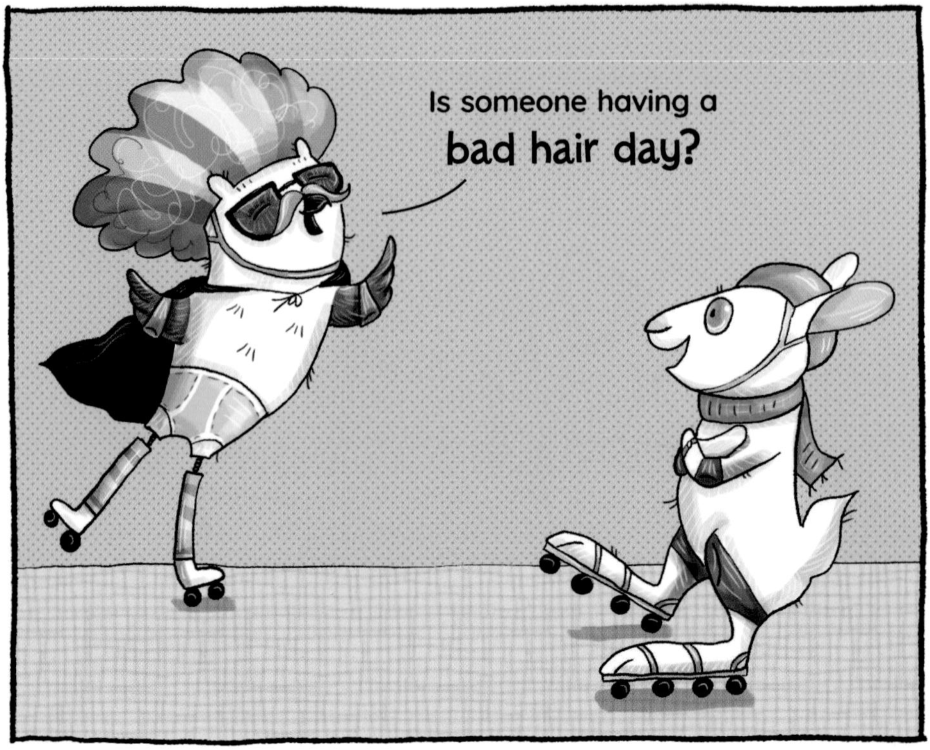
Is someone having a bad hair day?

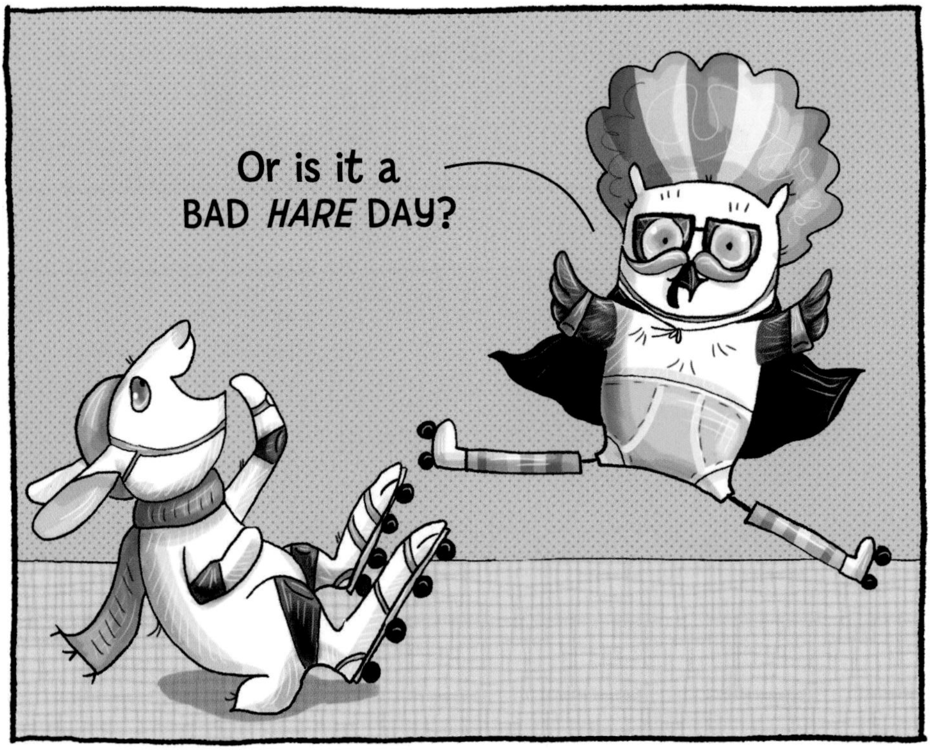
Or is it a BAD *HARE* DAY?

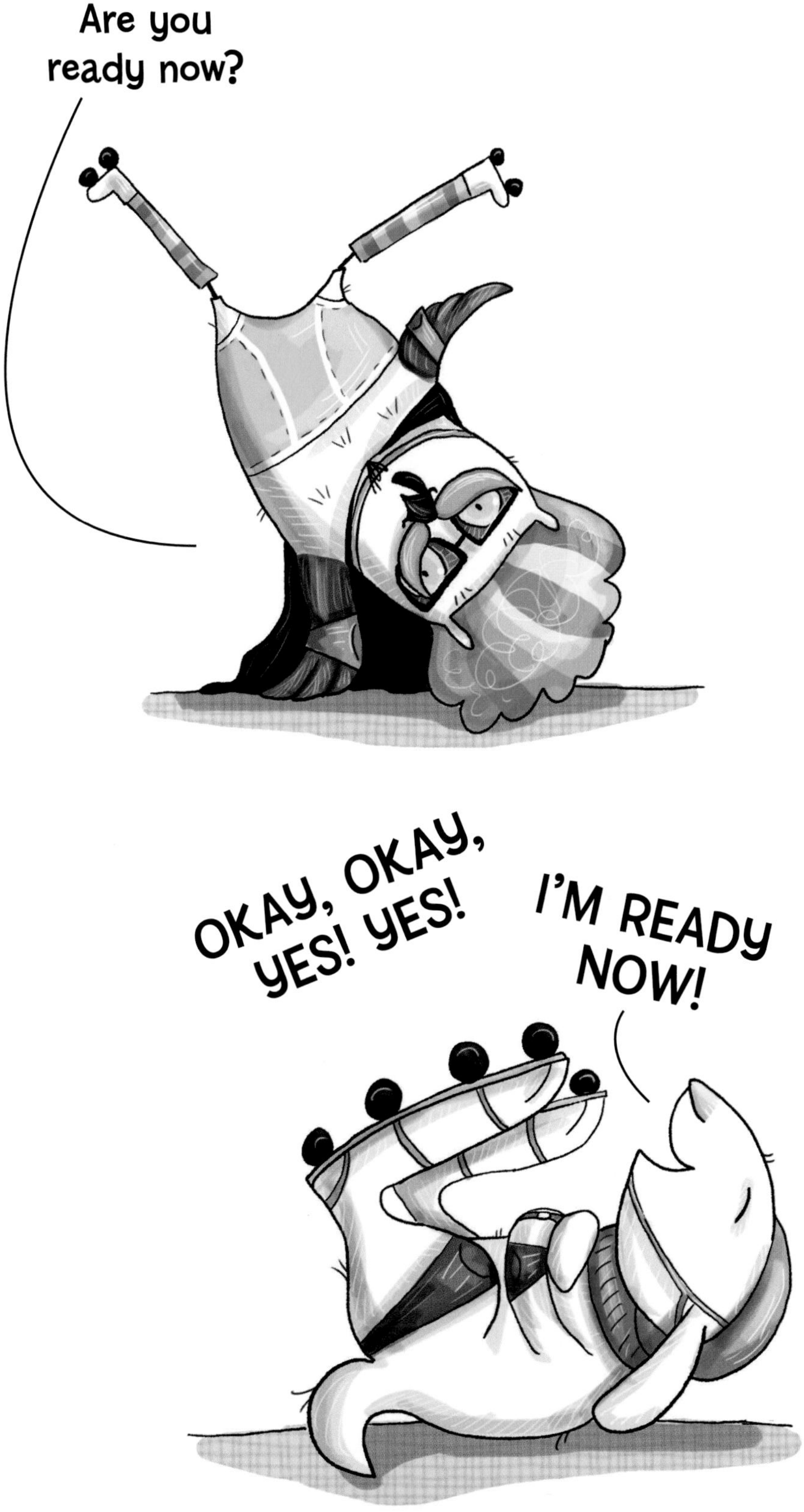

Are you ready now?
OKAY, OKAY, YES! YES!
I'M READY NOW!

CHAPTER 6
IT'S *OWL* GOOD!

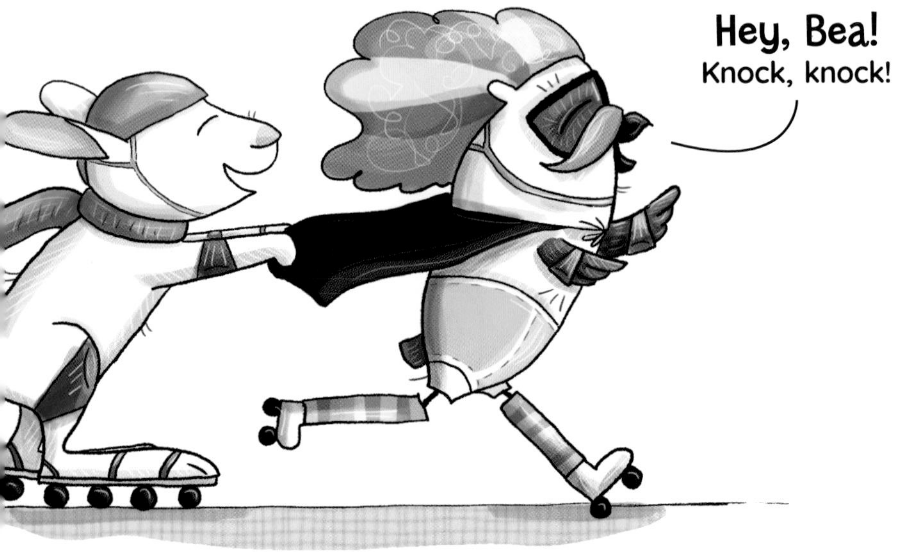
Hey, Bea!
Knock, knock!

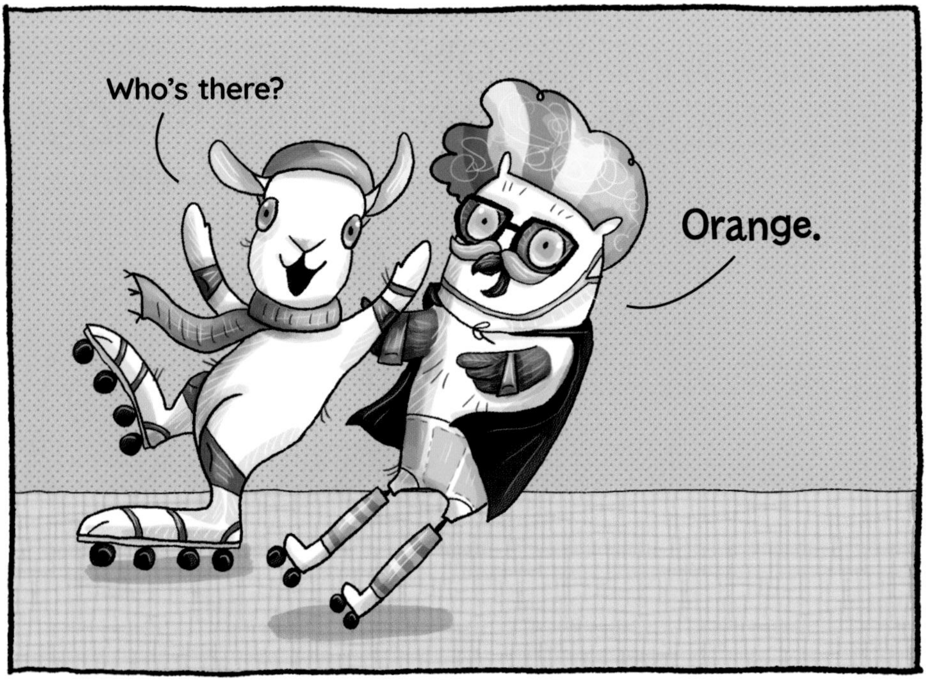
Who's there?
Orange.

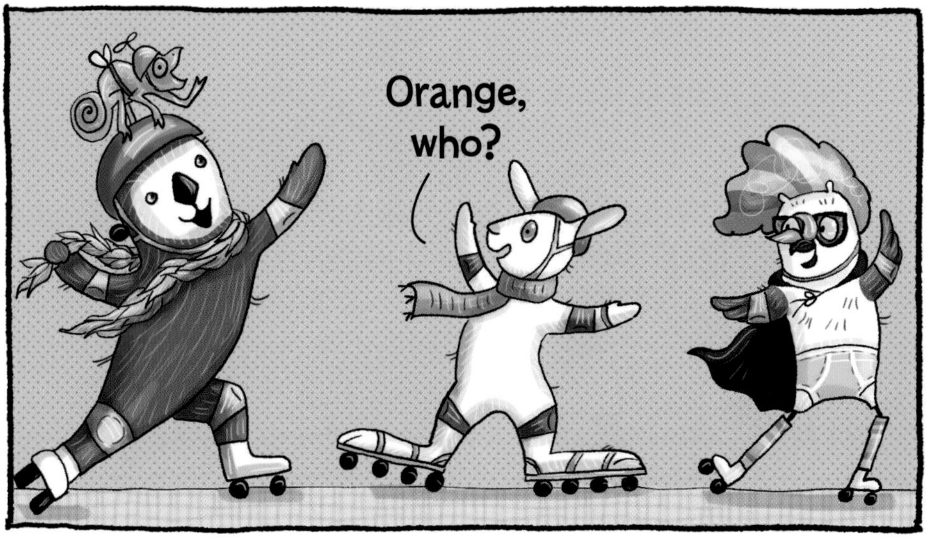
Orange,
who?

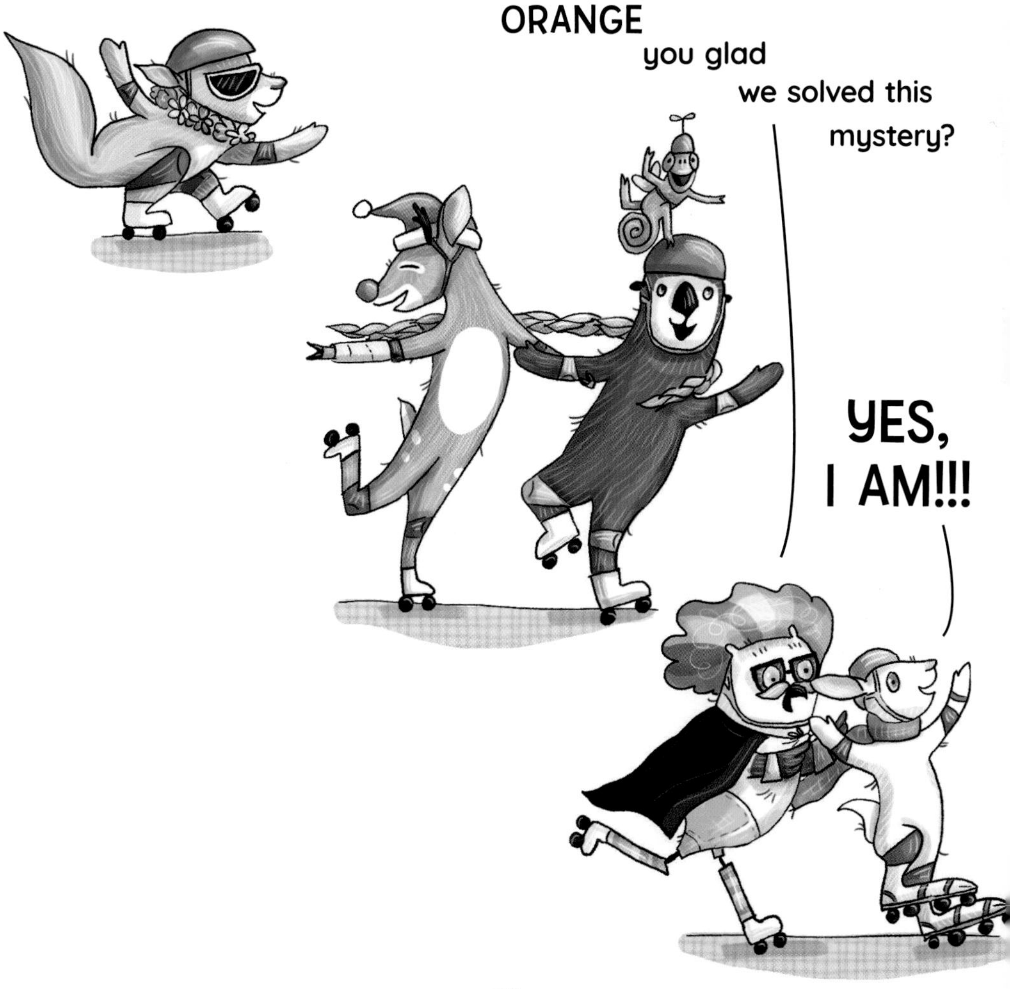
ORANGE
you glad
we solved this
mystery?
YES,
I AM!!!

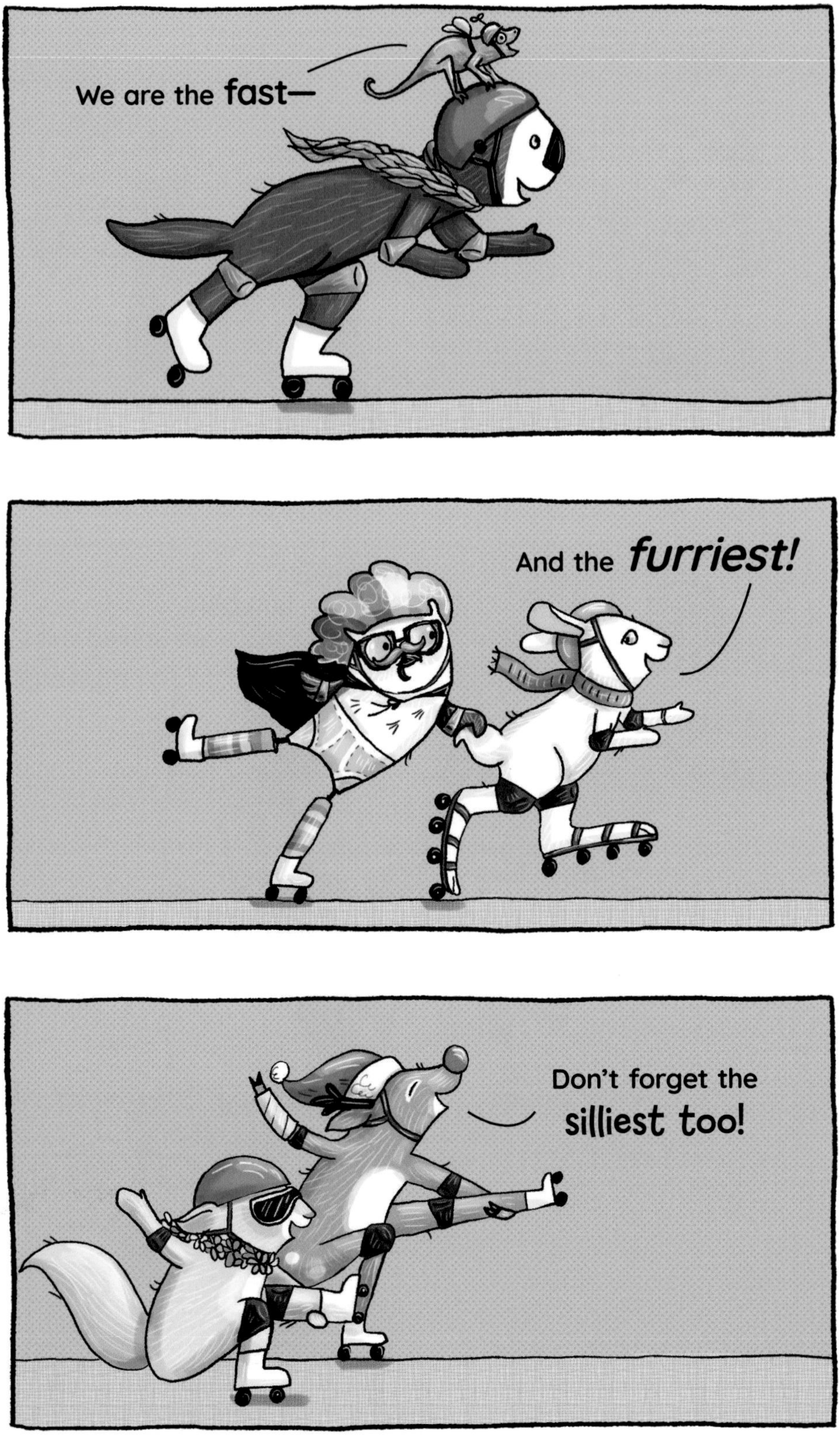
We are the fast—
And the furriest!
Don't forget the silliest too!

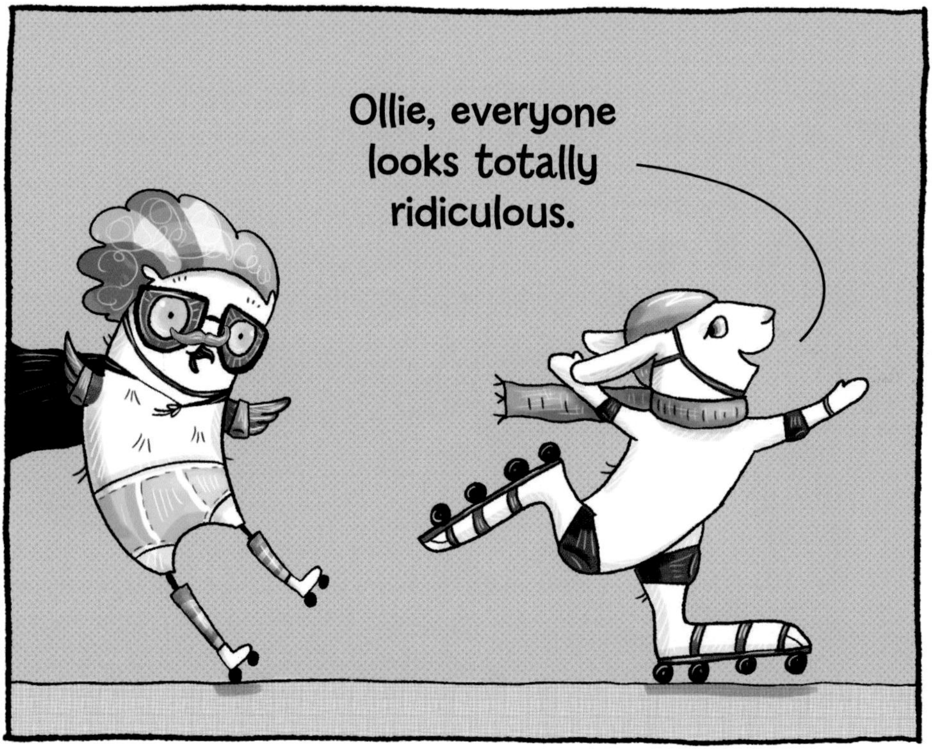
Ollie, everyone looks totally ridiculous.

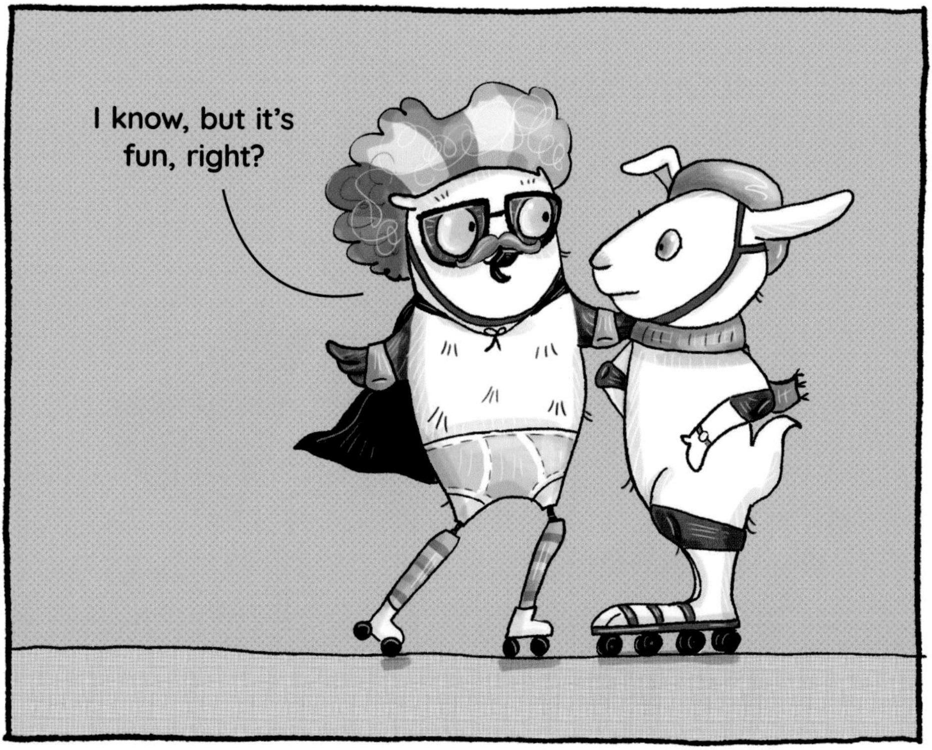
I know, but it's fun, right?

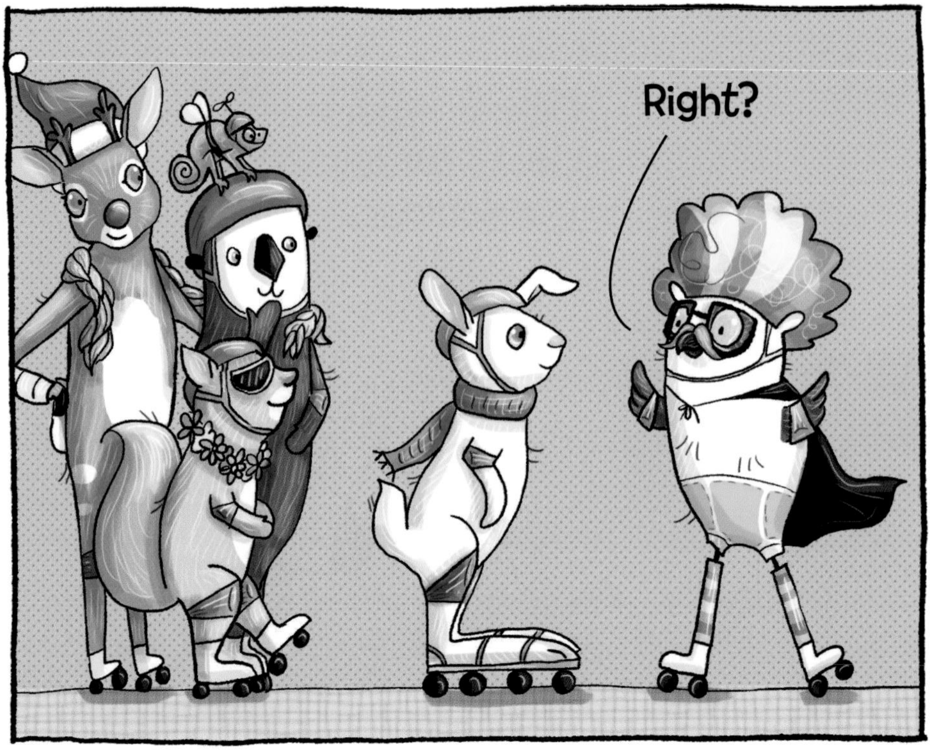
Right?

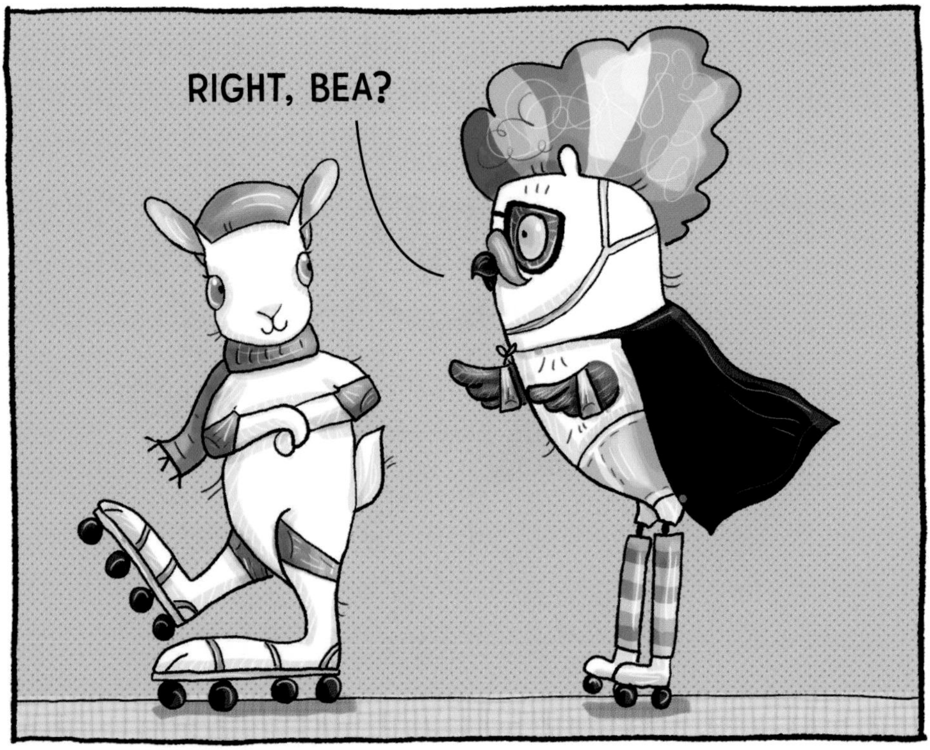
RIGHT, BEA?

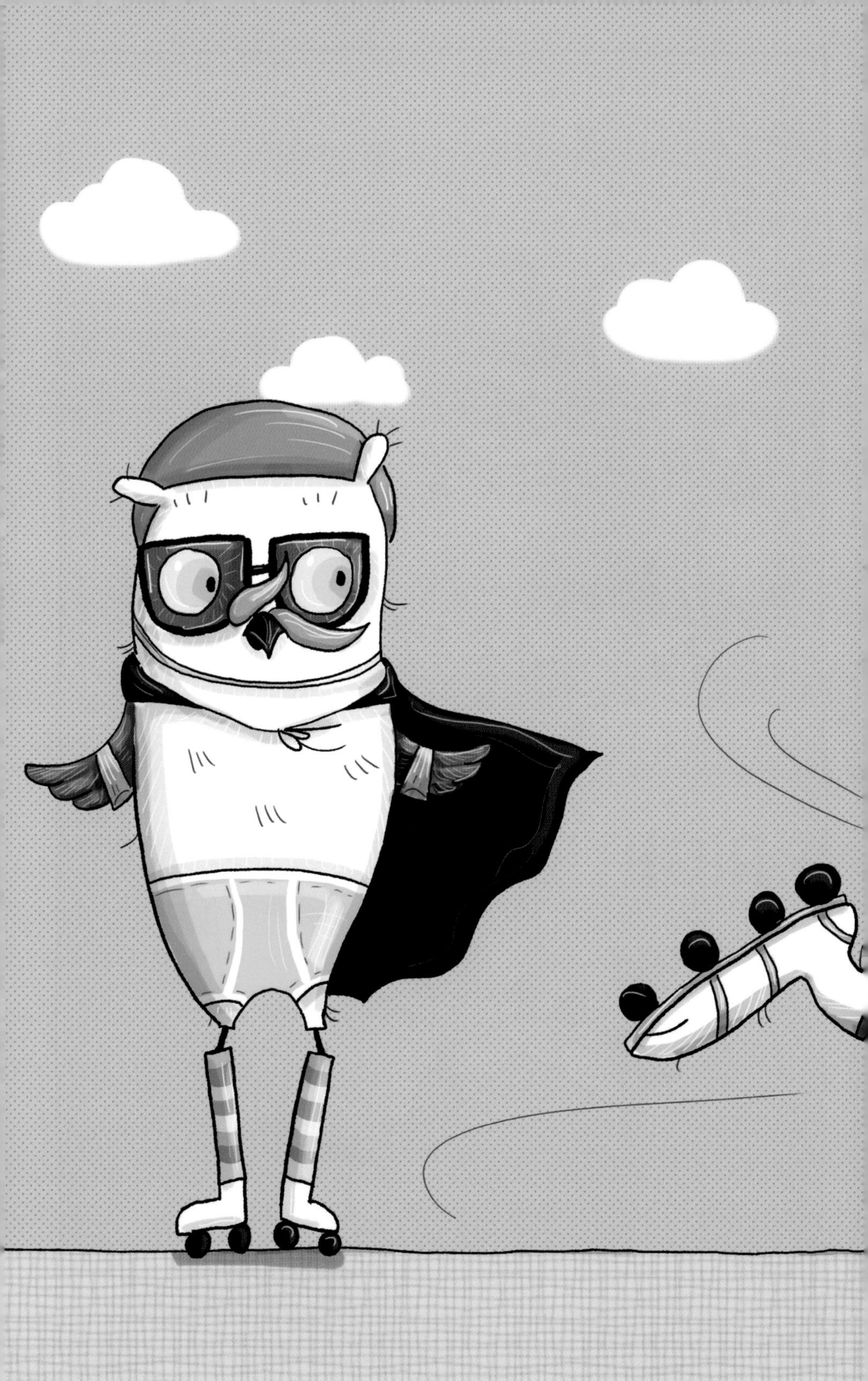

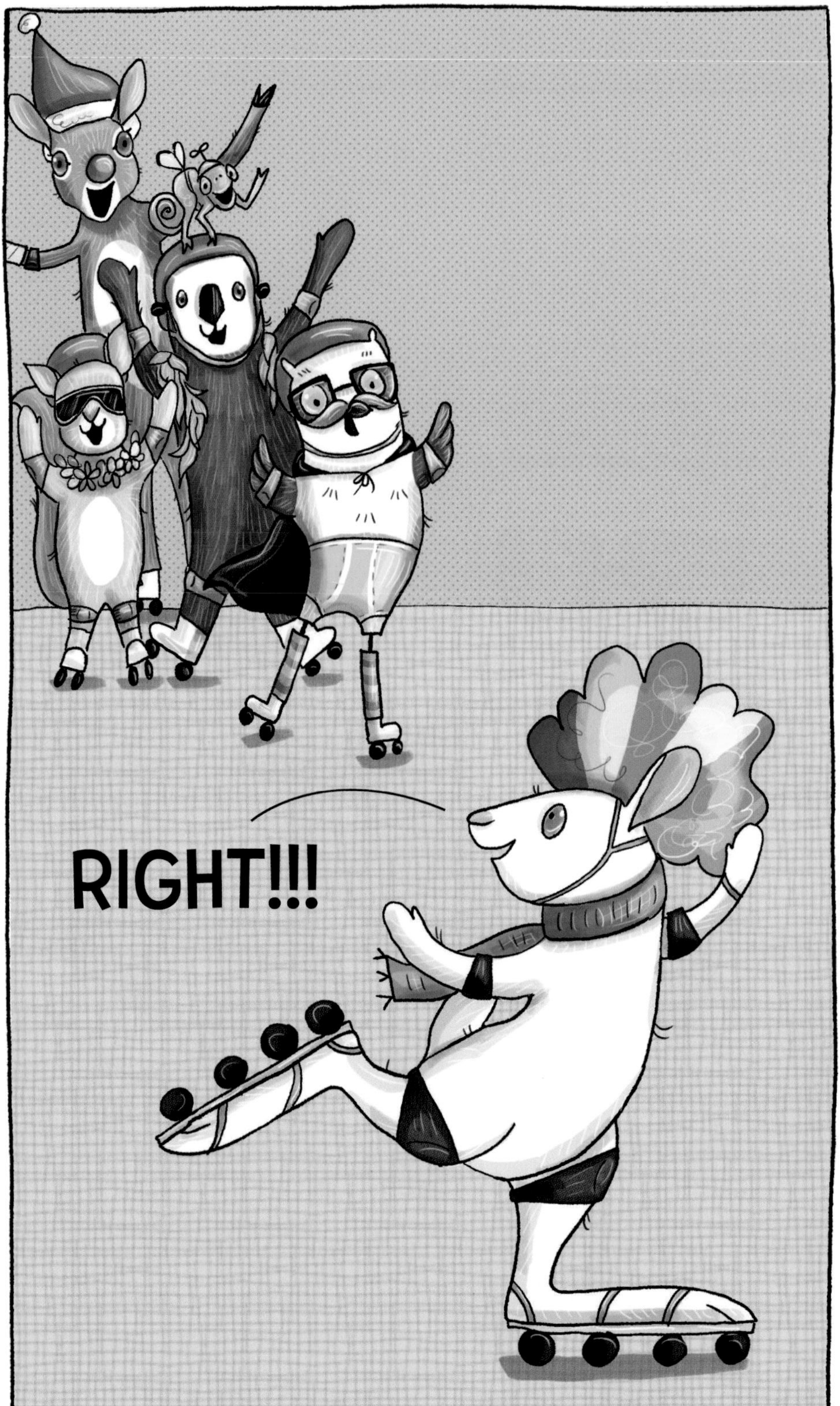
RIGHT!!!

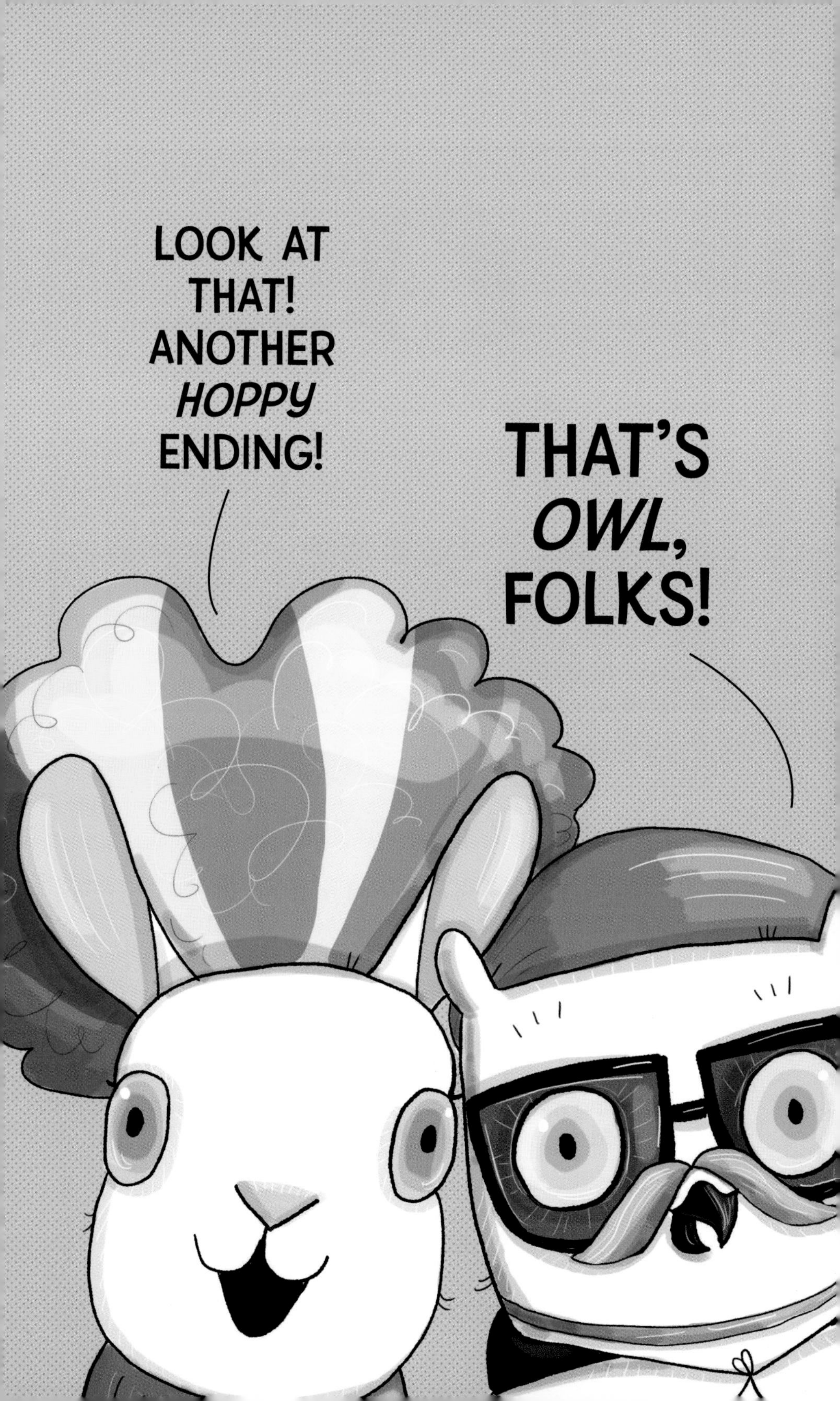
LOOK AT THAT! ANOTHER *HOPPY* ENDING!
THAT'S *OWL*, FOLKS!

ABOUT THE CREATOR

Renée Treml was born and raised in the United States and now lives on the beautiful Surf Coast in Australia. Her stories and illustrations are inspired by nature and influenced by her background in environmental science. When Renée is not writing or illustrating, she can be found walking in the bush or on the beach, or exploring museums, zoos, and aquariums with her family and superenthusiastic little dog.